A Death for the Records

North Dakota Library Mysteries
Number 3

ELLEN JACOBSON

Editor: UnderWraps Publishing

Cover Design: Molly Burton

Ebook ISBN: 978-1-951495-58-9
Paperback ISBN: 978-1-951495-65-7
Large Print ISBN: 978-1-951495-66-4

For anyone who has ever dreamed about setting a weird and unusual world record.

CONTENTS

Chapter 1
Avoidance Through Baking

Certain books should come with warning labels like, "Caution: this contains a lot of twists that will have you turning pages well past midnight," "Danger: this is about scary monsters and will give you nightmares," or "Beware: this cute romance will keep you up all night wondering why Hudson didn't kiss you goodnight on your first date."

By the time I finally drifted off to sleep, I still couldn't figure out why Hudson had ended our date so abruptly. I probably wasn't going to find out anytime soon since he's been back home in Florida taking care of a family emergency for the past several weeks.

I got a couple of hours of sleep before the loud squawking coming through my bedroom window woke me up. Why hens felt the need to announce the fact that they'd just laid an egg was something I still haven't sussed out. I rubbed my bleary eyes and checked the clock. Realizing it was already after seven, I jumped out of bed.

After taking a shower and getting ready, I resisted the temptation to find out what the cute couple in my insomnia-inducing read got up to next. But the sparks flying between the two lovebirds and their snarky banter would have to wait. Patting the book affectionately, I promised it I'd be back to keep it company later tonight. Then I headed down the stairs to my grandparents' kitchen.

It's weird calling it my *grandparents'* kitchen instead of *my* kitchen. Except for college and my stint living in Minneapolis, I've lived in this house practically my whole life. When my parents died in a car accident, my brother, Leif, and I were just young kids. Our grandparents took us in and raised us without hesitation.

Now, I was getting ready to move out and into my own place over Memorial Day weekend. It's hard to believe that it was less than a month away. Getting used to referring to this place as my grandparents' and not mine would be bittersweet for sure.

But I was grateful to have finally found a place in town within my budget. There had been an oil boom in western North Dakota during the past couple of decades. The resulting influx of workers had made it hard to find affordable housing. So, being in your late twenties and still living at home wasn't that uncommon for our neck of the woods. Of course, I hadn't been in a rush to leave my grandparents' warm and cozy farmhouse. If you've ever eaten my grandmother's cooking, you'd know why.

When I pushed open the door to the kitchen, Grandma was pouring freshly brewed coffee into a thermos. After screwing the lid on, she smoothed down her light pink cardigan and smiled at me. "Your grandfather has been in the barn since four. Do you mind running this out to him, Thea? There will be some breakfast casserole waiting for you when you get back."

The aroma of sausage wafting from the casserole dish as it sat upon a cooling rack on the counter was tantalizing. Inching closer, I exclaimed, "Oh, good! It looks like you put extra tater tots in it."

"When you get back, dear," Grandma said as she shooed me away. She tucked a couple of rhubarb cookies into a plastic bag. Glancing back at me, she added a few more. "I suppose you'll want some, too."

"Good thing Leif is away at that police training course, otherwise there wouldn't be any left for Grandpa or me," I teased.

"Don't worry, I'll make another batch when he gets back."

Studying my grandmother as she tucked the thermos of coffee, bag of cookies, some cups, and napkins into a wicker basket, I noticed the dark circles under her eyes. She lacked her usual sparkle. "You're still worried about Grandpa, aren't you?"

Grandma waved my concern away. "Uff da."

"Seriously, how are you?"

"Not too bad, dear."

I sighed. 'Not too bad' was what members of the Olson family always said. The house could be burning down, you could have a hundred and twenty degree fever, or the guy you had fallen for didn't kiss you goodnight on your first date, the answer would still be the same. No matter what internal emotional conflict you were going through, health issue you were dealing with, or external tragedy you were enduring, if anyone asked you how you were doing, the correct response was, 'I'm not too bad.'

Maybe that's because we're Scandinavian-Americans. Stoicism is second nature to us. Talking about our feelings wasn't done. But bottling everything up inside takes its toll after a while. I'd learned this the hard way, that's for sure.

Not knowing what to do, I motioned to the rocking chair in the corner of the kitchen. "Why don't you put your feet up for a while, Grandma?"

She shook her head. "Don't be silly, dear. I have a lot of cleaning to do. I want this place to be spick and span for our visitors. The clock is ticking after all."

From the tone of her voice, I could tell she was mentally capitalizing 'visitors,' turning it into a proper noun. These weren't ordinary guests we were expecting. In a little over forty-eight hours, officials from the McGuinness Book of World Records were going to descend on our small town of Why, North Dakota to determine whether my grandfather's giant ball of twine was the world's largest ball of twine. If it wasn't, my grandfather would be devastated. We'd all be.

It's no wonder Grandma hadn't been able to sleep. When a loved one's dream was on the brink of either being fulfilled or crushed, you couldn't help but be anxious.

Sure, Grandpa's dream was a bit unusual, but it had been years in the making. Tying strands of twine together one by one took a certain kind of commitment. I'd watched his ball of twine grow over the years, practically taking over the barn. What started as an idle hobby had turned into his obsession, one that's worthy of the title, 'The World's Largest Ball of Twine.'

"Go on, dear. Take this out to the barn." My grandmother thrust the wicker basket into my hands. "I'll keep the breakfast casserole warm for you."

As I made my way through the backyard, past the chicken coop and raised garden beds, I thought about how my ancestors had immigrated to this part of North Dakota from Norway in the 1800s. They had been a hardy bunch, leaving everything behind to start a new life out in these desolate parts. Their stoicism had probably served them well, helping them eke out an existence while enduring freezing cold winters. The large red barn was a testament to my family—sturdy and practical. But they were also a whimsical people, as evidenced by the large hand-carved wooden troll statue standing watch nearby.

After pausing to rub the troll's belly for good luck, I entered the barn and placed the basket on a makeshift table fashioned out of a piece of plywood and two sawhorses. My ankles were immediately ambushed by Loki and Bjorn, the two Pomeranians my grandfather had adopted when one of our town's prominent citizens passed away.

"Hang on a minute, guys," I said to them and rummaged in the basket. As I suspected, Grandma had also packed a treat for them—homemade peanut butter dog biscuits. Holding them up in the air, I ordered, "Sit."

Loki sat right away. As usual, Bjorn took a little while to settle down, doing a few excitable circles around my legs. Once Bjorn had taken his place next to his brother, I handed each of them a treat.

When they finished eating, I heard my grandfather call out behind me, "Twine."

While the dogs raced over to the corner of the barn, I turned to look at Grandpa. He was wearing his usual uniform—overalls, work boots, and a hat from the local feed store. Unlike my grandmother, his blue eyes were sparkling, and he seemed full of energy. I guess spending your early morning hours tying pieces of twine together would do that to you.

"Coffee?" Grandpa nodded at the basket.

"Uh-huh. And some cookies, too."

By this point, Loki and Bjorn had returned with twine clenched in their mouths and their tails wagging. "Give," my grandfather commanded. After the dogs deposited the twine into his hands, he pointed at the dog beds in the corner of the barn, and the pair trotted off to them obediently.

Grandpa was a man of few words. His new canine companions were ideal for him. They only needed one-word commands. No lengthy, in-depth conversation required.

"Here you go." I handed my grandfather a cup and sat next to him on a hay bale. We drank our coffee and munched on the rhubarb cookies in companionable silence.

"All set for the McGuinness folks to arrive?" I asked between sips of coffee.

My grandfather nodded.

"Anything I can do to help?"

Grandpa slurped his coffee, then shook his head.

I was about to ask if he had measured the ball of twine this morning when Denton Watts burst into the barn, shaking his fist in the air.

"Thor, I'm giving you one last warning," Denton shouted. "Call off this ridiculous event or else."

"Nope," Grandpa said after a moment's consideration.

I looked back and forth between the two men as they stared each other down. They were both up there in years and were dressed like twins with their overalls and feed store hats, but that's where the similarities ended.

Grandpa was on the shorter side with a potbelly that gave testament to my grandmother's tasty cooking. 'Scrawny beanpole' was how I would describe Denton. Squinty brown eyes with a perpetual sour expression on his face made people want to keep their distance. Unfortunately, since Denton owned the neighboring farm, we saw him far more often than we wanted.

"You're making a show of yourself," Denton said, jabbing a finger at my grandfather.

It was generally hard to read what Grandpa was feeling from his face, but there was a brief flicker of concern in his eyes. Denton had zeroed in on his weak spot. The last thing my grandfather ever wanted was to be in the spotlight. He'd be horrified if anyone thought he wanted personal fame and glory.

The giant ball of twine had taken on a life of its own over the years. It was almost like it had become a person in its own right, a trusted companion. And to Grandpa's mind, *it* deserved the world record, not him.

"I warned you about this," Denton said as he advanced toward my grandfather. "If you're not going to keep these world record folks from coming ... well, then I'm going to have to do something myself about it."

Shaking his head slowly, Grandpa said, "Gosh darn it, Denton. Nothing you can do about it."

Denton paused mid-step, and his brow furrowed. It was a pretty long speech for my grandfather, about as wordy as he gets, so I could see why he was surprised. Only then did his expression darken. Reaching into his overalls, Denton pulled out a pocketknife and flicked it open.

"I sure can." Denton slashed the knife back and forth in the air. "I can take a few inches off that precious ball of twine of yours."

Perhaps it was foolish, but I jumped in between Denton and the ball of twine. "Hang on a minute," I said, holding my hands up.

"Get out of my way, blondie," Denton said to me. "I got no beef with you. This is between your grandpa and me."

"Don't come another inch toward the ball of twine." I folded my arms across my chest in warning. "If you have a problem with my grandfather, then you have a problem with me."

Loki and Bjorn joined forces with me, barking ferociously at Denton. They were clearly trying to tell the scrawny man that the entire Olson clan—canine and human—had my grandfather's back.

Our combined forces must have intimidated Denton. He took a step in retreat and put his knife away. Next, he reached into his other pocket and pulled out a packet of jerky. Tearing off a couple of pieces, he flung them on the ground in front of the dogs. "Tangerine turkey teriyaki," he informed them. "It's my new recipe."

The Pomeranians wolfed it down in seconds, then looked up eagerly at Denton for more.

"Traitors," I muttered under my breath.

Denton turned to face my grandfather. "I'm warning you, Thor, call it off or it might not be so much the ball of twine you have to worry about."

***

Between bites of the breakfast casserole my grandmother had dished up for me, I filled her in on Denton's threats. Spearing a tater tot with my fork, I relayed how I had stood between the ball of twine and Denton. "Can you believe it? He actually said, 'Get out of my way, blondie.'"

Grandma took a sip of her coffee. "Well, you do have blonde hair."

"Yes, and I have blue eyes like Grandpa and I'm tall like you," I said. "But that's not the point. The point is Denton was brandishing a knife. A knife! He wanted to destroy the ball of twine. And he was going to go through me to do it."

"I see."

"You seem awfully calm about this." I leaned forward. "Don't you think we should report this to the police?"

She waved a hand in the air. "Denton is harmless. Don't pay him any mind."

"Grandma, don't you remember what happened when that couple from Williston wanted to lease some acreage from Grandpa?"

"They were a sweet couple, weren't they? The wife gave me a great recipe for banana chocolate chip bars. I haven't made those in ages." Grandma got up from the table and started rummaging through the cupboards. "I think I have some chocolate chips in here."

As I grabbed the dishes from the table and walked over to the sink, I reminded my grandmother that Denton had hammered nails into the tires of that nice couple's truck. "He's not a nice man."

"I recall there wasn't any proof Denton did that," my grandmother stated as she set containers of flour and sugar on the counter. "I should have a bag of bananas in the freezer. Can you get it out for me, dear?"

"Grandma, are you doing your baking avoidance thing again?"

"We're almost out of rhubarb cookies," she said matter-of-factly.

"Well, that's true." I was torn. On the one hand, chocolate chip banana bars sounded scrumptious. But on the other hand, I knew what Grandma was doing. When she didn't want to talk about something, she baked. Ensuring our mouths would be too full of sugary treats to keep asking her questions she didn't want to answer. "Tell you what, why don't I help you make the bars after we sort out what to do about Denton?"

"There's nothing to sort out. Maybe Denton went too far with the knife, but he was never going to hurt anyone."

"And the nails in the tire?"

My grandmother pressed her lips together and shook her head slowly. "I just can't believe Denton would do such a thing. Those nails could have gotten in the tire some other way."

"But I saw Denton sneaking around our driveway when Grandpa was out showing the couple the fields they were interested in leasing." I leaned against the counter and folded my arms across my chest. "I don't understand why you have such a soft spot for him. What is it you're not telling me about him?"

The doorbell rang before I could press my grandmother for an answer. "Go see who that is, please," she said to me before pulling open the freezer.

When I opened the door, Grace Ryan, the owner of the local newspaper, *The Daily Why*, was standing on the stoop with her phone pressed to her ear.

"How many times do I have to tell you? I'm not giving you a raise. You're lucky you even have a job," Grace screeched at the unfortunate person on the other end of the line. She held up her finger, motioning for me to wait. "Deadlines aren't suggestions. When I give you an assignment, I expect you to turn it in on time."

I stood awkwardly waiting while Grace continued to berate her employee. She certainly wasn't going to win 'Boss of the Year' anytime soon. No matter how poorly someone performed on the job, that was no excuse for swearing at them.

For a brief moment, I thought about giving Grace my business card and offering my services as a leadership coach. She certainly could use some management training. Fortunately, I had a full roster of clients—people who were pleasant to work with and actually wanted to improve their employee engagement, not destroy it. When Grace returned from New York City to take over from her father three years ago, she had burned through the newspaper's loyal workforce without remorse. Whoever was on the other end of the phone was just her latest victim.

Grace ended the call and smiled at me sweetly. "Good help is so hard to find. You're so lucky to be a one-woman shop, Thea."

"Actually, I've been thinking of hiring a virtual assistant," I told Grace.

"Ah, someone who can work remotely from home," she said. "That's smart. Then you don't have to deal with them in person. I wish I could do that with my staff. They're such a whiny bunch."

"Huh," I said simply. It wasn't worth telling her what I really thought. Grace was the type of woman who preferred people to parrot back what she said. Opinions contrary to what she believed were dismissed out of hand. "What can I do for you, Grace?"

"I need to talk to your grandmother. It's urgent." My eye was drawn to Grace's designer purse as she tucked her phone inside it. The neon orange leather popped against her tailored lime green pantsuit—a color combination that might look trendy on the streets of the Big Apple. Though it was out of place in a small town in western North Dakota. Yet, my own fashion sense tended toward the classic, comfortable, and unremarkable end of the spectrum.

"She's in the middle of something," I said, knowing my grandmother wasn't Grace's biggest fan. You shouldn't write an editorial advocating cuts to the library's budget and drop by the former library director's house unannounced, demanding to speak to her. "Can I tell Grandma what it's about?"

"It's a private matter." Grace pushed her way into the house and called out, "Rose? Rose? Are you here?"

My grandmother walked out of the kitchen, drying her hands on a towel. When she spotted our visitor, Grandma arched an eyebrow. "Grace. What an unexpected surprise. I thought we made ourselves clear the other day. Thor isn't interested."

I shot my grandmother a look. "What happened the other day?"

"Grace wants to do a hatchet job on your grandfather."

Holding her neon orange purse in front of her as though the bright color might ward off the glare coming from my grandmother's eyes, Grace said in a placating tone, "I would never do a hatchet job on Thor."

"Really? I thought you specialized in hatchet jobs," Grandma said. "Your last article nearly put the Little Pickle out of business. You had people convinced they were tinkering with the expiration dates on products and passing them off as still good. Thankfully, someone realized that the photos you published in the paper were fake. There aren't many people with six fingers on their hands working at the Little Pickle."

"But that wasn't me," Grace protested. "I fired the reporter once I found out the story was made up."

"That's not what he said," my grandmother countered. "He claims you pressured him into writing it and generating those fake images. It was either that or lose his job. And it's not the first time something like this has happened to someone who worked for you. Is it any wonder you're facing multiple lawsuits?"

Grace narrowed her eyes. "The courts will side with me. You'll see. Disgruntled employees are a dime a dozen."

"Clickbait, sensationalist journalism isn't how you're going to get the newspaper out of the red," my grandmother said coolly. "Your father built the newspaper from the ground up based on sound principles—honest and accurate reporting coupled with celebrating the community we live in."

"Exactly." Grace seized on what my grandmother said. "That's why I want to interview Thor—to celebrate his achievement. A story about the world's largest ball of twine, here in our own hometown, could make the national news."

"And there it is." Grandma gripped the dishtowel in her hands tightly. "You want to write about Thor for your own personal glory."

Grace put a hand to her chest. "This story will be good for everyone. It will put Why on the map."

"You know, my grandfather isn't exactly a verbose guy," I said, trying to lighten the mood. "Any interview you did with him would consist of only a few words—'yep,' 'nope,' and 'you betcha.' I'm not sure this story would be worth your time."

Grandma chuckled. "Thea's right. Interviewing Thor would be like squeezing blood out of a rutabaga."

"Well, at least let my photographer take pictures of the ball of twine," Grace said.

"Nope." Grandma shook her head. "Thor has an agreement with the folks from the McGuinness Book of World Records. They are the ones who have the exclusive right to photograph the ball of twine until the judging is complete."

"I think you mean the Guinness Book of World Records, not McGuinness," Grace said.

"No, I mean McGuinness," my grandmother said acerbically. "For goodness' sake, if you want to write a news report about something, at least get the facts straight. Everyone knows that it's the McGuinness folks who are coming out here, not the Guinness ones."

Grace looked genuinely dumbfounded. "I'm sorry, I don't—"

"You obviously didn't do any basic research before calling on us to try to badger Thor into being interviewed. So, I guess I'll have to explain it to you. The McGuinness organization was established a couple of years ago to provide a new and unique approach to certifying world records."

"Really? What do they do that's so special?" Grace asked.

"They wear costumes based on the theme of the record being set," my grandmother explained.

Grace furrowed her brow. "Costumes?"

"And they do a song and dance number during the judging process," I added.

"Okay, let me see if I've got this straight. The judges are going to dress up as what ... balls of twine? And do a performance number about twine?"

I nodded. "And they stream it."

"So, basically, McGuinness is a rival organization that does some sort of mash-up of *America's Got Talent* and a failed Broadway musical," Grace said skeptically. "And your grandfather agreed to this? The man who doesn't like to draw attention to himself. He's going to participate in a mini musical about a ball of twine, but he won't agree to an interview by *The Daily Why*?"

"Yeah, that about sums it up," I said. What I didn't tell her was that when Grandpa sent a letter about having his ball of twine certified as the world's largest, he didn't realize that he had sent it to the McGuinness organization rather than the Guinness Book of World Records. By the time any of us had figured out that he was dealing with the former rather than the latter, the arrangements had already been made. To be honest, I didn't think he cared who did the judging. Grandpa simply wanted someone other than himself to measure the ball of twine and confirm it was indeed the world's biggest.

"How much are they paying you?" Grace asked.

My grandmother shook her head. "They're not paying us a dime."

When Grace gave her an incredulous look, I said, "All the money is going to the 'Farm to Food Bank' charity. Maybe that's what you should write about. It could help raise money for them, too."

Grace scoffed at the idea and gave us an evil smile. "I have a much better idea for a story. Tell Thor he's going to wish I had interviewed him instead."

After Grace turned and walked out of the house, my grandmother and I exchanged looks.

"Are you as worried as I am about what Grace is going to write about?" I asked her.

"I have more important things to worry about," Grandma replied. "Like getting those banana chocolate chip bars made."

My grandmother's tone might have been cheerful, but the look in her eyes told me otherwise. I needed to find a way to stop Grace before she did too much damage.

CHAPTER 2
IT'S FIELD TRIP TIME

When I walked into the library later in the afternoon for my volunteer shift, I was still in a foul mood. This morning's events were overwhelming—Denton Watts pulling out a knife and threatening to destroy Grandpa's giant ball of twine, followed by Grace Ryan barging into the house demanding an interview with my grandfather. When thwarted, she'd promised to write an article in *The Daily Why* that he would regret.

Normally, spending a few hours shelving books or helping the staff with programs was relaxing and enjoyable. It also didn't hurt that the guy I had started to develop feelings for, Hudson Carter, was the library's current director. We'd always found some time to chat while I was at the library. Whether it was swapping book recommendations, chuckling over the antics of Hudson's cat, Dr. McCoy, or reminiscing about the murder cases we had cracked, the time always flew by when Hudson and I were together.

Today was a different story. The lights in Hudson's office were off—a sign that he was still in Florida with his family while I was here in North Dakota alone and worried about my grandfather.

"How's Thor feeling about the big day?" one of the library assistants asked me.

"He's doing well," I admitted with more confidence than I felt.

"Tell him we're all rooting for him." The library assistant pointed at a large plastic container crammed full of twine on the checkout counter. "People have been coming in here all week dropping off bits of twine for your grandpa. They all want to know that their twine is part of the 'Whymonstrosity.'"

"The 'Whymonstrosity?'"

The library assistant shrugged. "That's what folks have been calling it. Kind of catchy, don't you think? Anyway, do you mind taking this container with you when you leave tonight? It's so full, I'm going to start another one."

"No problem." I nodded over at the full book cart. "Am I on shelving duty today?"

"Sure are." As I started to push the cart toward the Collingsworth Wing, the library assistant stopped me. "Actually, there's a fellow here who was hoping to have a word with you. Where did he go … Oh, there he is. The bald guy over by the computer stations."

I furrowed my brow. "What does he want?"

"Something about a book he's writing."

As I neared the man in question, noticing the nicks and cuts on the back of his scalp, I wondered if he was new to shaving his head or if he had used a really dull razor. Hudson had a full head of dark, wavy hair. What would he look like bald? The look definitely suited some guys, but I couldn't imagine not being able to run my fingers through Hudson's hair … not that I had ever done so. But you never know, maybe one day.

Geez, I was starting to annoy even myself with my ridiculous lovelorn nonsense. It was time to stop reading romance. While I was shelving books, I was going to have to keep an eye out for something to take my mind off Hudson. Hard sci-fi maybe? Nothing like a battle in space and the threat of an alien invasion to distract oneself.

Lightly tapping the man on his shoulder, I said, "Excuse me, sir. You were looking for me? I'm Thea Olson."

He sprung to his feet and turned to face me, his expression a mixture of curiosity and wariness. It reminded me of the poor stray cats at the Humane Society—wanting to explore the world but scared of how it might treat them.

"M-m-miss Olson," he stammered, holding out his hand. "It's nice to meet you."

His grip was surprisingly strong, almost a little too firm. When I finally extricated my hand, I said, "And you are?"

"I am?" The man scratched his head, which was probably a mistake given all the cuts on his scalp. I think he realized that too. He quickly withdrew his hand and shoved it in the front pocket of his jeans. "What ... am I?"

Worried he thought we were playing some sort of children's riddle game, I quickly added, "Your name. What's your name?"

"Oh, sorry." He started to scratch his head again, but stopped his hand mid-air. "I, uh, haven't had any coffee today. I'm a little fuzzy."

Okay, well that was understandable. If I went for more than two hours without a cup of coffee, I'd be a little fuzzy myself. Coffee flowed through the Olson family's veins. Giving it up was unthinkable.

"So, your name is ..." I prompted.

"Ivan Koslov," he said. Then he repeated it even more slowly, "Ivan Koslov."

"Got it. Nice to meet you, Mr. Koslov."

"Please call me Ivan," he said.

I nodded. "So, what can I do for you, Ivan?"

"Did the man at the desk explain that I'm a writer from, um, Florida?"

"He did."

"Did he explain about the book I'm working on?"

I shifted back and forth on my feet, wishing this overly drawn-out conversation would wrap up. "No, sorry, he didn't"

Ivan looked crestfallen. "Oh, I thought he would have."

"Why don't you explain it to me?" As the words escaped my mouth, I instantly regretted it.

A smile crept across the bald man's face. "I'd love to."

"Actually, I just realized I need to get these shelved." I motioned toward all the books on my cart. "Maybe you could just explain what you need to speak with me about?"

"It's about twine."

"You wanted to talk with me about twine?"

"No ... I mean, yes." Ivan scratched his head again. "My book is about twine. That's what I want to talk to you about—your family's ball of twine."

"The 'Whymonstrosity?'" I couldn't believe how easily the new moniker for Grandpa's giant ball slipped off my tongue. The library assistant was right—it was catchy.

"Yes, exactly. I'm traveling around the country doing research for my great American novel. Could anything be more quintessential when it comes to describing the American spirit and essence than a giant ball of twine?"

I couldn't argue with him. A solitary man working away, in an often freezing cold barn, tying piece after piece of twine together for no other reason than to see the ball of twine get bigger and bigger? Well, that certainly signified a certain dogged perseverance. Probably an odd and quirky one at that, but a determination, nonetheless.

"Everyone says you're the person to talk to, Miss Olson."

"Please call me Thea," I said.

"Thank you, Thea," Ivan said, reaching over to squeeze my fingers. I shuddered. He was clasping my hand with his hand—the same one that had been scratching his cut-and-scrape-covered head.

"I knew you could help," he continued. "When would be a good time for me to come over and interview your family?"

"Oh, no, I'm sorry. You misunderstood. My grandfather isn't interested in being interviewed."

Ivan's eyes widened. "But my book will be incomplete without an in-depth account of the 'Whymonstrosity.'"

"I'm sorry," I said. "Maybe after the official judging process, but certainly not now."

The man's shoulders slumped. "I thought people in North Dakota would be friendlier than the people in Minnesota."

I tilted my head to the side. "What do you mean?"

"They wouldn't talk to me either."

Probably because you come across as a strange little man, I wanted to admit. But I refrained, instead simply giving him a sympathetic look.

"That's okay." His expression brightened. "I'll just work my questions through the McGuinness people."

"You've been in contact with them?"

"Uh-huh. I told them all about my book. They were very excited. I'm meeting Mr. Shafer when he arrives to discuss my becoming an official member of the judging delegation."

"Really." I made a mental note to get to Mr. Shafer first and explain my reservations. I'm sure Ivan meant well. Clearly, he's obsessed ... No, wait a minute. Let's go with 'keen' not 'obsessed.' It's a much nicer way of describing Ivan's interest in giant balls of twine. I couldn't really go around thinking people who wrote about giant balls of twine were weird, could I? After all, what would that make people who actually made giant balls of twine, like my grandfather? Even weirder?

I sighed. There were times I wished Grandpa had taken up a more normal hobby like whittling wood or bird-watching. But then he wouldn't be Thor Olson, would he?

Ivan gathered up his pile of papers from the computer station and shoved them into his messenger bag. "I've got to go," he told me. "Lots of prep to do before I meet Mr. Shafer."

"Um, okay."

He gave me a little wave and scurried away. As he dashed through the main entrance door, I wondered if Ivan giving up coffee was such a good idea. Perhaps if he indulged in a latte or a cappuccino, he might be a little less awkward. Caffeine could give you a real confidence boost.

Feeling a slight headache coming on, I rubbed my temples before I pushed the book cart toward the nonfiction section. I spent the next twenty minutes happily putting books where they belonged, pausing occasionally to peruse the back covers and leaf through the pages of books that caught my eye.

But my mood soured again when I picked up the next book off the cart—*The Dehydrator Bible*. Naturally, it reminded me of Denton and his passion for dehydrating fruits, vegetables, fish, meat, and baked goods, not to mention non-animate objects. He enjoyed putting together unusual flavor combinations. Some worked out better than others. Personally, I do not recommend his tuna fish blueberry muffin jerky. Crumbly blue fish with a hint of sugar and vanilla? No thanks.

As I was placing *The Dehydrator Bible* next to *The Guide to Dehydrating for Fun and Money*, I heard a whooshing sound behind me. It was followed by a familiar voice with a thick New York accent calling out to me. I groaned. Please, please, please, I implored the universe. This day had been bad enough as it was. Please don't let that be Edgar.

"Hey, lady. I'm talking to you," I heard the raspy voice say again. "Stop ignoring me. I know you can hear me."

I groaned. It had been two weeks since Edgar had last made an appearance. Fourteen quiet days without having to deal with my nemesis. But I knew if I ignored him, he'd make my life miserable. Clenching my fists into balls, I turned and looked at the bookshelf where the spiritual guide that the library had bestowed upon me was perched, waiting for me. Only I could see and hear him, and he was supposed to help me when I needed it. Instead, he only gave me snarky advice and cryptic clues when I was trying to solve murder cases. The chameleon had been magically transported from New York City to a small library in North Dakota.

"Hi, Edgar," I said glumly. "What do you want?"

"I want to get out of here, lady. I've been trapped in this library for ages. It's driving me bananas. You gotta help me escape."

"Escape? To where?"

"Where else?" Edgar rolled his eyes. "To your grandfather's barn. I want to see this giant ball of twine everyone is talking about."

***

Focusing on shelving books, I tried my best to ignore Edgar after his ridiculous request to take him on a field trip to my family farm. I wheeled the cart between the stacks. But every time I paused to place a book on a shelf, the obnoxious chameleon materialized.

"Watch yourself," I warned when he came dangerously close to having a hefty tome of Icelandic poetry land on his tail.

He flicked his tail out of the way, then asked if I preferred Eddaic or Skaldic forms of poetry.

"I don't know what you're talking about."

"Maybe you should borrow the book and learn the difference, lady. I've seen what you've been checking out lately." Edgar rolled his eyes in that particularly disturbing way he did—an eye in one direction, the opposite eye in another. "All those kissy-kissy, smooching books. Gross."

"How do you know what I've been checking out? Library records are supposed to be confidential."

"I have my ways." He gave me the reptile equivalent of a shrug. "Don't you think it's time you got over Hudson? If he really cared about you, he wouldn't have run away to Florida. He's probably not coming back."

"He didn't run away." I placed my hands on my hips. "It was a family emergency. He's coming back."

"How do you know that? Did he text you? Call you? Do the two of you stay up all night talking on the phone like teenagers saying, 'You hang up first,' 'No, you hang up first,' 'No you,' 'No you,' ... blah, blah, blah, until one of you falls asleep?"

"That's none of your business!" I snapped. Hudson had only sent me a few short texts, and we had one extremely brief conversation, but I wasn't going to tell Edgar anything. Wait a minute ... if Edgar could somehow hack into the library system with his strange magical powers, did that mean he could also hack my phone? Did he read my texts?

Edgar let out a particularly loud belch. Belching wasn't something I knew chameleons could do until I met this particular lizard. Or maybe only magical reptiles belched, and ordinary, run-of-the-mill chameleons didn't? If only there were some sort of handbook on how these mysterious guides worked.

I cocked my head to the side. Hang on. Maybe there *was* a handbook. I'd have to ask my grandmother about it when I got home. Like all the women in our family since the founding of the Why library, Grandma had also been bestowed a guide. Hers was an adorable Angora rabbit—not that I had ever seen it. Spiritual guides were only visible to and interacted with their assigned humans.

From what my grandmother had told me about her guide, the rabbit was kind, sweet, and encouraging. Grandma wouldn't have needed a handbook. If she had questions, the rabbit guide would have answered them.

Mine, on the other hand, was a snarky chameleon. I'd swear he was an 80-year-old curmudgeon who had been chain smoking since he was old enough to steal cigarettes from his mom's purse. Who was I kidding? A handbook on how to deal with this obnoxious reptile didn't exist. I was on my own.

"If your hunky library director does come back, I hope he leaves that stupid cat back in Florida," Edgar said.

"What's wrong with Dr. McCoy?" I asked.

"He's a cat."

"And you're a chameleon," I replied, stating the obvious.

"Exactly." Edgar hopped onto a stack of books on my cart. "Let's get back to our field trip. Will you be providing snacks?"

"What is with you and snacks?"

"Do you know how much energy is required to vanish and reappear?" As if to prove his point, Edgar disappeared with a loud whooshing sound.

Moments later, I felt something strike the back of my neck. Whirling around, I spotted the chameleon lounging on a shelf directly behind where I had been standing. "Gross. Did you just stick your tongue on me?"

"I was trying to catch a fly. I missed," he said nonchalantly. "Like I told you, I need to refuel after moving through the time and space thing. Do you happen to have a hot dog on you? Man, I'd give anything to be back in New York City, where you can find a decent hot dog on every street corner."

I patted my pockets. "Does it look like I'm carrying around a hot dog in here?"

"Maybe you need bigger pockets," Edgar suggested. "Girls are always complaining about the size of the pockets on or in their clothes, or the lack of pockets altogether. You should buy yourself something with extra-large pockets, so you can keep a stash of hot dogs in them for me."

"Uh, no." I furrowed my brow. "Hang on a minute. I know you travel through space." I pointed to the book cart where Edgar had previously been and then back to the shelf he was currently on. "But did you also say travel through time? Can you go to the future?"

"Geez, lady! I'm not giving you the winning lottery numbers if that's what you're asking."

"No, I don't want the lottery numbers."

"Really," Edgar said dryly. "You don't want to become a multi-millionaire?"

"Well, sure, that would be nice …" my voice trailed off as I thought about what I could do with all that money. Make a hefty donation to the library, that's for sure. Take a trip to Europe definitely. Better yet, take my entire family to Norway and explore where our ancestors had come from. We still had cousins living there. It would be fun to finally meet them in person.

"Earth to blondie," Edgar called, interrupting my day-dreaming. "You're not getting the lottery numbers, and that's final. It's not how this works."

"Okay, so explain. How does this all work?" I waved my hands in the air, lowering my voice when I heard someone walking past the stacks. Once I was sure they were out of earshot, I said, "You were magically transported from New York City to this library to be my guide, right?"

"Yep, that sums it up." Edgar did his own waving of hands, mimicking me. "I've been banished to this place where you can't find a decent hot dog."

"You like the nacho dogs from Swede's Diner," I reminded him.

"They'll do in a pinch," he huffed. "But they're nothing compared to a dog smothered in sauerkraut and mustard from the Big Apple."

"Can we get back to the time travel thing, please?" I asked, trying to ward off yet another one of Edgar's long diatribes about the inferiority of North Dakota hot dogs.

"Look, I barely understand how it all works, lady. How do you expect that you, a mere human, could possibly comprehend it?"

"A mere human?"

Edgar let out a low growl. "Here we go again. Just because *Homo sapiens sapiens* have opposable thumbs doesn't mean your species is better than the rest of us. Can you snap your fingers and change color? Go on, try it. I'll wait."

I pressed my temples. Edgar's condescension wasn't doing anything to help my headache.

"No. Can't do it. Pasty white is your only color option? Here, let me show you how it's done." The air in front of me blurred for a moment. When my eyes were able to focus again, Edgar was now iridescent purple instead of his previous blue-green coloring. He held up one of his arms and examined it. "Not bad, not bad at all." He fixed his beady eyes on me. "They say purple is a sign of royalty."

"Oh, for Pete's sake. Do not expect me to start curtsying."

"A simple bob of the head will do, lady."

"Hah! That will be the day." I turned around and pushed the book of Icelandic poetry into place, making sure its spine was aligned with the others.

"I thought you were checking that out," Edgar said.

"Nope," I said, although I was secretly intrigued by the cover.

Edgar hopped back onto the cart and looked up at me. "We should start our book club up again."

"No way. That was a disaster. You read what you want to read, and I'll read what I want to read. And we'll keep our thoughts about our books to ourselves. Deal?"

Ignoring what I said, Edgar flicked his tongue out again, trying to catch another fly. When Hudson got back, I was going to have to talk with him about the flies in the library.

If he comes back, the little voice of insecurity inside me said.

I mentally shook myself. *Hudson is coming back.*

"Hey, lady. Finish shelving these books and then meet me in the break room. I want to check out your purse."

"I don't have any hot dogs in it."

"How about some peanuts?"

"There are no snacks in my purse," I said firmly.

"Chill, lady. It was worth a shot. But that's not why I want to see your purse, anyway."

Thankfully, Edgar left me alone while I finished shelving books. When I returned the cart to the front desk, the library assistant asked if I could fold some flyers for an upcoming children's program. "I've got it all set up for you in the break room. You can have a cup of coffee while you work."

Little did he know, the last thing I wanted was to go there and deal with Edgar. But no one else knew about my guide except my grandmother. So, there was little point in telling the library assistant that a snarky chameleon was waiting to ambush me in the break room.

A pile of flyers was waiting for me on the table, along with Edgar.

"Where's your purse, lady?"

Sometimes it's just easier to give in, and this was one of those occasions. I walked over to the locker I'd used and pulled out my bag. "Here," I said, holding it up.

"Bring it closer. My eyesight isn't what it used to be."

"Exactly how old are you?" I asked, setting the purse on the table.

Edgar sniffed the brown leather and flicked his tongue at the zipper. "Open it."

"What's the magic word?"

"Now."

I scowled at Edgar, ignoring his demand, and walked over to the coffee station. After selecting a hazelnut pod and popping it in the machine, I heard a tiny voice pleading, "Please."

Whirring around, I pointed at the chameleon. "Did you just say 'please?'"

"Don't push your luck, lady. Open the darn purse."

With a grin plastered on my face at having made the reptile bend to my will, I unzipped it. Edgar burrowed inside. After a lot of grumbles and grunts, he tossed some cough drops out, followed by a quarter. Finally, he emerged from my purse and glared at me.

"This won't do."

"Well, I don't know what to tell you. It's a perfectly fine purse. I've had it for ages."

"It's ugly, but that's beside the point." Edgar jumped up onto the pile of flyers. "Go home and ask your grandmother for the bag with a tapestry lining. She'll know what I'm talking about."

"Want to enlighten me before I proceed with your request?"

"Lady, do you care about your grandfather at all?"

"Of course I do ..." I spluttered. "What does a purse have to do with him?"

"Geez, enough with the questions already. Get that bag from your grandmother, or else you'll be sorry!" Edgar snapped before the whooshing noise started and he disappeared yet again.

Chapter 3
The Troll Without a Name

I ignored Edgar's obnoxious demand to find some stupid tapestry-lined bag. Like I was really going to bug my grandmother about a bag just so Edgar could get out of the library for a few hours. It was all hands on deck getting everything ready for the arrival of the McGuinness representatives. A small part of me was almost convinced that Edgar was genuinely concerned about my grandfather, but I brushed it aside. Edgar was interested in it only for himself. This was all about getting out of the library, not helping my family. Was I just being stubborn? Maybe. But as far as I was concerned, guide or no guide, Edgar could stuff it.

And anyway, the library clearly thought the snarky chameleon was the bee's knees. Otherwise, why would it have mysteriously transported him from New York City? The library could keep the chameleon entertained. Edgar likes to read, and the library has tons of books. They were a match made in heaven. I imagined Edgar running around on the farm creating havoc—the opposite of heaven. Edgar could stay where he belongs—prowling around the stacks and keeping the fly population in check.

The next day went by in a blur, helping my grandparents get everything ready for the arrival of the McGuinness representatives. Grandpa focused on making sure the barn was spick and span, with the occasional break to add more twine to the 'Whymonstrosity.'

The kitchen was my grandmother's domain. From her command center, she was organizing the reception that would be held in the barn the day after tomorrow at the conclusion of the official judging event. Local dignitaries would be attending, including Why's mayor, our state representative, and the newly crowned Miss Prairie Dog, along with our friends and family.

Fortunately, Grandma was too busy managing all the logistics of the event to dwell on the possibility that the McGuinness judge might measure the ball of twine, then turn and give my grandfather a sympathetic look before informing the assembled guests that the 'Whymonstrosity' was only the *second* largest ball of twine in the world. Rather than a celebratory reception, we would be hosting a pity party.

No, who am I kidding? Worry was etched in my grandmother's eyes. It was the same concern I saw in my own eyes. She just didn't talk about it, and taking my cue from her, neither did I.

Instead, Grandma was furiously whipping up dishes that would keep, as well as planning out the rest of the menu for the reception. Not a pity party, a reception, as I kept reminding myself. The usual classics would make an appearance, such as dill pickle roll-ups, sweet and sour meatballs, and deviled eggs. But my grandmother was also testing some new recipes, and that was where I came in. Between running to the Little Pickle to pick up groceries and getting the punch bowls out from the basement, I was the official taster. To be fair, the dogs considered them-selves official tasters as well. They were constantly under-foot, ready to sample anything that fell on the floor.

The tater tot nachos she made were amazing, but you really couldn't go wrong with tater tots, could you? They were definitely on the menu. My favorite though had to be Grandma's new cake pop recipe—cake crumbs formed into balls, coated in melted chocolate, and covered in light brown frosting, which my grandmother drizzled in stripes to resemble strands of twine. They were going to be the hit of the party. Miniature sugary balls of twine. Yes, please.

"Thea, be a dear, and go see if your grandpa wants a sandwich," my grandmother said to me, interrupting my thoughts. "He's barely eaten all day, which isn't like that man."

Knowing we could use an extra helping of good luck, I made sure to stop by the wooden troll statue first. "Troll," I said, wondering again for the millionth time why no one in our family had ever gotten around to giving him a proper name. Calling the troll 'Troll' seemed a bit rude, not to mention unimaginative. But that was a problem for another day. "If you could help make sure everything goes smoothly tomorrow, I'd appreciate it."

As usual, Troll didn't respond. A true tribute to his Scandinavian stoicism. But I could swear I saw a twinkle in his eyes, which was ridiculous. I shook my head. Not that long ago, I would have laughed if anyone had told me a mysterious talking chameleon would live in the library that only I could see. Now that I had accepted the fact that Edgar wasn't imaginary, I was starting to think other things were real, like this large troll statue in front of me. Carved wooden eyes shouldn't twinkle. *It's the sunlight, that's all,* I told myself firmly. It's not a real troll. The only place those beasts exist are in books or movies.

Of course, I rubbed the troll's belly for good luck before continuing to the barn. The troll might not be real, but it couldn't hurt, right?

When I poked my head through the door, I saw Grandpa at his workbench. He was intent on something and didn't hear me come in, so I took a moment to look around the barn. Toward the rear were stalls for livestock. When I was younger, we had a dairy cow for a brief spell. Though for the most part, the stalls had been uninhabited and used mostly for storing farm tools and implements, not to mention the occasional game of hide-and-seek with my brother and cousins.

Glancing upward, a smile crept across my face. I may or may not have had my first kiss in the hayloft with a boy who's now a dentist in Fargo. But my smile faded, remembering the non-kiss with Hudson. I took a deep breath, inhaling the slightly sweet, musty odor of the barn, and let it out slowly, trying to release my anxieties.

Turning to look around the barn, I noticed how neat and tidy Grandpa had made everything. Dirt had been swept off the rough wooden floors, hay bales were neatly stacked, and folding chairs and tables had been set up for the reception the day after tomorrow.

My gaze lingered on the main attraction—the 'Why-monstrosity' taking pride of place in the center of the barn. It stood on a platform raised off the floor by a few inches, and my grandfather had erected a rope barricade around it, reminding me of an exhibit at a museum. All that was missing was a placard in front, declaring it to be the world's largest ball of twine.

Walking over to the workbench, I noticed my grandfather holding a large padlock. "What's that for?" I asked.

Grandpa nodded at me before he said, "Denton. Gate."

It took me a moment to decode what he meant. "It's for the back gate to keep Denton from driving up to the barn uninvited?"

"Yep."

There were two ways to get to the barn. One was on foot, walking from the house through the garden—the route I had taken. The other access point was for vehicles, through a gate off the gravel road that ran alongside the property. When my grandfather had been actively farming the land, the gate had gotten a lot of use as he had made trips to and from the barn to the fields. Nowadays, Grandpa and most visitors usually walked to the barn from the house.

However, when Denton came by, he used the county road access point as it was closer to his own property. I bit back a smile. Grandpa had always left that gate unlocked. But Denton's unannounced and unwelcome visit the other day was too much. You didn't threaten a man's ball of twine with a knife, then expect to come and go as you please.

"Key. Blue." Grandpa pointed at the pegboard over his workbench.

"Got it," I said, noting a key hanging from a blue ribbon between a hammer and a pair of pruning shears.

He waved the padlock in the air. "Gonna lock it."

"When you're done, head to the house. Grandma's got a sandwich for you." Noticing a stack of half-folded paper on the side of the workbench, I added, "I can finish these up."

Grandpa patted my shoulder, then left to go barricade the gate against Denton. I sat down on the stool and spent the next several minutes folding pieces of paper in half to create pamphlets for the event. My brother, Leif, had designed them, putting into words the history behind our grandfather's hobby turned all-consuming passion. The story highlighted how members of the community had participated as well, by either contributing scraps of twine or helping to tie them on.

My eyes got misty as I examined the photos Leif had included, my gaze lingering on the one of our parents. They stood next to Grandpa in front of the then much smaller ball of twine.

A woman shrieked, cutting through the silence. I threw down the pamphlet and rushed in the direction of the voice to see if she was okay. As I approached the barn door, the woman said firmly, "Cut it out, Wolf. How many times do I have to tell you I don't like it when you do that?"

Silhouetted in the doorway was a couple—a man of average height with a belly that protruded over his khaki pants and a tall, slender woman with dark hair that flowed to her waist. He had his hand on her arm, trying to pull her closer.

I was about to intercede when the woman's voice took on a more playful tone. "That is unless you want to buy me that convertible I have my eye on."

The man reached around and gave her a swat on her rear end. She giggled in response. He gave her an indulgent smile. "Darling, you know I can't buy you a car right now."

Even though this was my family's property and these strangers were intruding on me, I decided to give the two lovebirds some privacy. I started to step back, but then the man added, "Until my divorce goes through, my hands are tied." I hated to admit I was drawn into wanting to know more about their little soap opera. Tucking myself behind some bales of hay, I listened. Eavesdropping wasn't exactly an admirable trait, but I couldn't help myself.

The woman's voice turned steely. "You promised we would be married by now."

"Kayla, sweetie," he pleaded. "Cool it, please. I'm under enough pressure as it is. And you know that. Let's just get through this, okay?"

"I can't believe you dragged me to this godforsaken place," she complained. "Why couldn't you have gotten a sexier assignment, like giving out the world record for the largest bottle of wine in the south of France? Instead, I have to smile at a bunch of yokels and pretend to be interested in a stupid ball of twine."

"Play nice, Kayla," the man said. "We're only here for a few days."

It took me a moment to realize that I had clenched my fists. How dare that horrible woman speak about North Dakota and my grandfather that way? I was going to give her a piece of my mind. But then I groaned, realizing that the two people speaking were official representatives of the McGuinness organization. Not only would that woman have to play nice, but, if I didn't want to sabotage my grandfather's shot at the world record, I needed to be on my best behavior as well.

***

I unclenched my fists and plastered a smile on my face, steeling myself to 'play nice' with that despicable woman.

But just as I emerged from behind the hay bales to greet the philanderer and his girlfriend, they flung themselves into each other's arms, kissing and loudly moaning. Apparently, they had confused the entrance to the barn with the doorway to some seedy motel room.

Turning around, I crept back over to the workbench and busied myself again with the pamphlets. Thankfully, I couldn't hear their amorous entanglement from where I sat. There's something creepy about a man close to retirement age groping a much younger woman.

As I placed the completed pamphlets in a stack on the side of the workbench, I wondered if Grandpa had already made his way back to the house for a bite to eat. It couldn't have taken him that long to put a padlock on the gate. I chuckled. What if my grandfather had stumbled across the two officials from McGuinness mid-embrace? Public displays of affection generally made him uncomfortable. Knowing Grandpa, he'd probably clear his throat to get their attention, and just nod politely.

"Hello, anyone here?" I heard Wolf call out.

"No one's here," Kayla said to him. "I told you I saw that old geezer walking the other way. Did you see the overalls he had on? Honey, you should get a pair and dress up as a country bumpkin for Halloween this year. It'd be hilarious."

I should have gotten up from the workbench and made my presence known. But they couldn't see me from where they were, and some sort of sick fascination had taken over me. What other horrible things were going to come out of this gal's mouth?

Turns out I didn't have long to wait. "It really is a monstrosity, isn't it?" Kayla said.

Hmm. When local folks called the ball of twine the 'Whymonstrosity,' it sounded cute. But hearing it described as a 'monstrosity' by Kayla left a sour taste in my mouth.

"And it's dirty," she continued. "Look at how gross that twine is. Ugh! It stinks, too."

"Now, darling, remember what I told you," Wolf said. "Play nice."

"How about if we play footsie instead?" Kayla suggested.

Okay, I'd had enough. I couldn't stand to listen to Kayla's insults or her icky come-ons to Wolf anymore. I got up and walked around the ball of twine, pretending to take earbuds out and put them in my pocket. Looking up with feigned surprise, I said, "Oh, hello. I didn't know anyone was here. Must have had my music on too loud."

Kayla gave me a sickly sweet smile as she tucked a strand of her long dark hair behind her ear. Wolf's smile was more natural. Stepping forward with his hand extended, he introduced himself. "Wolf Shafer. McGuinness Regional Director, Head of Streaming and Licensing, Chief of Technology Innovation, and Vice President of Branding."

"Wow, that's quite a mouthful," I said, shaking his hand. "I'm Thea Olson. Granddaughter of Thor and Rose Olson, Sister to Leif Olson, Library Volunteer, and Owner of Thea Olson Consulting." As I released Wolf's hand, I added, "Oh, I forgot one. Official Pickle Taster."

"Why do you taste pickles?" Kayla asked with her brow furrowed.

"She was joking." Wolf wagged a finger at me. "Pickle tasting! You've got a good sense of humor. I like that in a girl."

"I wasn't kidding about the pickle tasting," I replied. "The Little Pickle—that's the local grocery store—is having a competition soon for the best pickle in the county. I was appointed to the judging panel."

"Better you than me." Kayla ran her fingers down her waist and patted her flat tummy. "All that sodium can make you bloated."

Wolf gave her a warning look, then introduced us. "This is my assistant, Kayla Goodwin."

She's more than just your assistant, I wanted to say. Somehow, I stopped myself. Instead, I held out my hand to her and received a tepid handshake in return. "Nice to meet you," I said with forced sincerity and turned back to Wolf. "I thought you weren't arriving until tomorrow morning. Not that it isn't nice to have you here now," I quickly added.

"Well, there was a screwup with the flights from Los Angeles," Wolf explained.

Kayla scowled at her boss. "That wasn't my fault. I wanted to—"

"Nobody is saying it's your fault," Wolf placated her. "This worked out better. We get to explore the nightlife in Why."

"Oh, goody," Kayla muttered under her breath.

"Um, Why isn't exactly known for its nightlife," I pointed out. "Bingo was yesterday, and the steak dinner at the lodge got canceled on account of the cook skipping town. If you want to stay in, the Little Pickle does grocery deliveries." I tapped my finger on my lip and smiled at them. "But the roller rink is having a retro theme night this evening. You can skate to music from the 70s, and there's going to be a competition for the best costume. Bell bottoms for the win."

"You people have a lot of competitions around here," Kayla said. I could tell she was holding back her sarcasm, but some of it still came through in her voice.

Wolf shot her a look and mouthed something. Probably, 'Play nice.'

I spread my hands out. "Isn't that the business you folks are in—the competition business? I would have thought it would be right up your alley."

Wolf seized on this. "You're absolutely right. We love competitions. Pickles, 70s costumes, giant balls of twine ... you name it, we love it."

Kayla looked dubious.

"I should get my grandfather," I said to Wolf. "I know he's looking forward to meeting you. He's most likely at the house grabbing a bite to eat."

"We should probably do the same. It's been a long day. Why don't we catch your grandfather tomorrow morning as originally planned?" Wolf said.

"Are you sure?" I asked. "You came all this way."

"All this way?" Kayla chuckled. "We're staying right across the road from you."

"Across the road? But the only thing across the way is the Larsens' place."

The cogs started to turn in my head as I remembered the Larsens hadn't returned from Arizona this year after spending the winter there. The older couple had become enamored with the warm climate and were thinking about selling their house here. Hudson had rented it earlier this year before moving into his own place. So, it was already set up for short and long-term rentals. Lucky me. Wolf and his lovely assistant, Kayla, were going to be my neighbors during their stay in North Dakota.

After saying as much to them—without the sarcastic 'lucky me'—I added, "I assumed you'd be staying in Williston. It's only about an hour away."

Wolf rubbed his hands together. "Nope, I like to be close to the action."

"Action. Humph!" Kayla said as she arched a perfectly manicured eyebrow. I raised a less plucked one back. Turning again to Wolf, I asked, "Did you walk across the road?"

He nodded. "Thought it'd be nice to stretch our legs. We stopped by the house and met your grandmother. Lovely woman. She pointed us toward the barn here. Anyway, we're gonna get going. You can tell your grandfather that we'll see him bright and early tomorrow morning."

"For the pre-judging assessment, right?" I asked.

"That's right." Wolf nodded. "We'll do a preliminary measurement of the ball of twine—"

My eyes widened. "So, you'll know tomorrow if it's the world's largest?"

Wolf held up his hand. "No, this won't be an official measurement. It's simply to calibrate our measuring equipment."

"We also need to finalize the choreography now that we've seen the ... um, performance venue," Kayla added. "The dancers will be arriving tomorrow afternoon for the dress rehearsal."

"That's right." Wolf clapped a hand on Kayla's shoulder, cutting her off. "There's a lot to do to get ready for a production of this size."

"But you'll know tomorrow, won't you ..." I pressed, "If the 'Whymonstrosity' is the world record-holder?"

Kayla wrinkled her nose. "'Whymonstrosity.'"

"Hmm, 'Whymonstrosity,'" Wolf mused. "That's catchy. We could do something with that in the marketing materials."

"But—"

Wolf looked me in the eye. "Young lady, I know you're eager to know what the outcome is. But I'm afraid the results of the pre-judging assessment will be confidential. In fact, we'll ask everyone to leave the venue while the measuring is underway. The only two people who will know the preliminary results will be Kayla and me."

I pressed my lips together, trying to keep the butterflies in my stomach from escaping. This waiting was nerve-racking, more so than my first job interview after graduating college.

"Alright then," Wolf said brightly. "We'll get out of your hair."

I walked back with them. Kayla appeared interested in the garden beds as we passed by them. "I tried growing sweet peas one year, but they died," she said. "I love how they smell."

"You should talk to my grandmother about it," I said. "She could give you some pointers."

Kayla smiled at me, a genuine smile this time. "Thanks. I'd like that."

When we had reached the front of the house, I asked Wolf again if they wanted to come in and meet Grandpa.

Wolf rubbed his abdomen. "Do you hear that rumbling? I've got to get some food in my belly." He turned to Kayla. "Maybe we'll hit up the roller rink after that. What do you say?"

"Let's talk about it after dinner," she said slowly.

"Try Swede's Diner," I suggested. "I think the special is Thai meatloaf tonight."

Kayla tilted her head. "Thai meatloaf?"

"Swede is into fusion food," I explained. "Some of the foods he combines aren't exactly compatible. But I've had the meatloaf before. It's tasty. Turns out curry paste, lemongrass, and ground beef are a good combo. But whatever you do, stay away from the Thai pie. Curry paste, turmeric, and cherry filling ..." I shuddered. "Best to avoid it."

After waving goodbye to Wolf and Kayla, I pushed open the front door and called out, "Grandpa, wait until I tell you about the McGuinness folks."

My grandmother walked out of the kitchen. "Your grandfather isn't here. Didn't you tell him to come back for a sandwich?"

"What? He should have been back ages ago." I shook my head. "Something must have happened with the padlock."

"Padlock?"

After explaining about Grandpa wanting to lock the gate in order to keep Denton away, I told her that I'd walk out there to see what happened.

As I passed by the bed of sweet peas, I thought about Kayla and how her whole manner had transformed when talking about gardening. It was hard to reconcile her with the mean-spirited woman who had trash-talked my grandfather and the 'Whymonstrosity.'

I paused for a moment to rub the troll's belly and then made my way around the barn. When I reached the gate, I frowned. It was wide open, and my grandfather wasn't anywhere to be seen. Turning back to the barn, I went inside and called out for him. When he didn't respond, I did a sweep of the barn, but he wasn't anywhere to be found.

Why would he go to put a padlock on the gate, but instead leave it wide open? I had overheard Kayla saying they had seen my grandfather walking the other way. At the time, I'd assumed she meant my grandfather had been walking on the path toward the house. But maybe she had seen him walking down the road instead? But why? Where would he go?

My mind whirred with possible explanations for his disappearance. When it even went as far as alien abduction, I shook my head. This was what happened when you solved a few murder mysteries. You imagined dramatic scenarios when there's really a simple explanation for what happened. Most likely, the lock wouldn't close, and Grandpa had been fiddling with it the entire time Wolf and Kayla visited with me. He probably came into the barn again for some WD-40 after we had left. But he couldn't find it, so he went to the house to check if any was in the basement.

Somehow, I'd missed him on the way back when I went looking for him.

But after trudging to the house and not finding Grandpa, my stomach clenched. I looked at my grandmother, who was calmly cleaning the coffeemaker. How was I supposed to tell her that her husband had disappeared?

CHAPTER 4
GLUTEN-FREE BUDDIES

The next morning, Grandma, Grandpa, and I were sitting at the kitchen table with coffee cups in hand, while we waited for Wolf and Kayla to arrive. A silence descended over the room, but not the easy, companionable one we usually had. It was a heavy silence, one that weighed on everyone. The arrival of the McGuinness folks was one of the biggest events in Grandpa's life. What if things didn't go to plan?

Grandma's spoon clattered as she stirred some more half-and-half into her cup. The cuckoo clock on the wall ticked. My grandfather slurped his coffee. The dogs snored softly as they lay in their doggie beds. My bracelets knocked against each other as I toyed with them. Every sound resonated in the space.

Finally, I couldn't take it anymore. Breaking the silence, I asked, "Grandpa, why won't you tell us where you disappeared to last night?"

"Told you. Went for a walk," he said.

"But you never go for walks." I pointed out the kitchen window. "There's no place nice to walk around here. It's a gravel road."

"People go speeding down it all the time," my grandmother added. "You have to be careful out there, especially at night."

"Exactly." I nodded, then checked myself. When had I become such a worrywart? Leif and I had walked down that same road all the time to go play with the neighbor kids. Looking at my grandfather, noticing the wrinkles around his blue eyes and the way he was rubbing his arthritic knee, I realized my worry was more about how old he was getting. What if he had gotten seriously hurt while he was out on his mysterious jaunt last night? Recuperating from a broken hip or worse wouldn't be easy at his age.

"Please, next time you want to go for a walk, let me know," I said. "I'll go with you."

The doorbell rang before he could argue with me. Grandma got up from the table and adjusted the silk scarf around her neck. "They're here. Thea, can you set out the cookies while I let them in?"

As my grandmother ushered Wolf and Kayla into the kitchen, Grandpa got to his feet. He adjusted the straps of his overalls as he walked over to shake Wolf's hand. Even the dogs yipped their own excited greeting at the visitors.

"Mr. Olson," Wolf said heartily. "It's a pleasure to finally meet you."

Grandpa nodded. "Yep, same." He turned to Kayla and tipped his hat. "Ma'am."

Kayla appeared disarmed by this display of chivalry. She smiled at my grandfather. "Please call me Kayla."

After everyone was seated at the table and fresh coffee had been poured, I passed the plate of almond cookies to Wolf. He placed a couple on his plate, then tried to hand it back to me.

"Kayla hasn't gotten any yet," I said.

"Oh, she's watching her figure." Wolf glanced at his assistant. "Isn't that right?"

"I'm not on a diet. I'm gluten free," she explained testily.

"I thought it was peanuts you couldn't eat," Wolf said.

Kayla pressed her lips together. "Peanuts *and* gluten."

Grandma frowned. "I'm so sorry, dear. If I had known, I would have made something else."

Kayla shook her head. "It's fine. Really."

"Hmm." My grandmother glanced at the hutch cabinet in the corner where her cookbooks were stored, obviously thinking about what gluten and peanut-free recipes she could make for Kayla.

"These cookies are delicious. Good thing Kayla can't have any. More for the rest of us." Wolf wiped crumbs off his mouth and set his napkin down. "Why don't we go through a rundown of what's lined up for today and tomorrow?"

"Okie dokie," Grandpa agreed.

"After we're done here, we'll go to the barn and have a more thorough look around," Wolf said as he snatched another cookie off the plate. Glancing at me, he asked, "Did you tell Thor that we visited the barn yesterday?" Wolf looked over at my grandfather. "Is it okay if I call you Thor?"

Grandpa nodded. "You betcha."

Wolf grinned. "I love how you say that. It's straight from that old movie *Fargo*."

My grandmother tsked. She was not a fan of *Fargo*—too much violence, swearing, and stereotypes of Minnesotans and North Dakotans for her liking. But the funny thing was that she'd watched it half a dozen times. I'm pretty sure it's because of her soft spot for Steve Buscemi.

"Anyway, we'll take a look at the barn and figure out how we want to stage things," Wolf said. "The dancers will be arriving around two for the dress rehearsal."

"We also need to check the lighting," Kayla explained. "It's pretty dark in there."

Wolf chuckled. "Kayla is scared of the dark."

Kayla flicked her hair back over her shoulders. "Oh, it's not the dark I'm scared of. It's when the sun comes up, you look over in bed and see your boyfriend lying there. Now, that's scary."

Wolf shot the woman a look. "What's that supposed to mean?"

"The guy I'm seeing is really old." Kayla gave us a tight smile. "All wrinkly like a prune. You know what I mean? And it takes forever for him to—"

"Kayla, that's enough!" Wolf snapped.

My eyebrows shot up at this exchange. Clearly, Kayla had no idea that I had witnessed her romantic interlude with Wolf yesterday. Otherwise, she wouldn't say such catty things about her lover. Or would she?

I glanced over at my grandparents. Grandma looked scandalized, and Grandpa stared down at his cup of coffee. Silence had descended on the room again, only this time it was the embarrassing kind. So awkward. Thankfully, the doorbell rang, giving us an excuse to talk about something else.

"I wonder who that could be?" my grandmother said as she stood.

Wolf snatched another cookie off the plate. "It's probably Ivan Koslov," he said with a forced cheerfulness. "He's a writer from Florida who's working on a novel about twine."

"A novel about twine?" Grandma paused in the doorway to the hall. "That's original."

"I met him yesterday at the library," I said before Grandma proceeded to answer the door.

"That's what he told me when we spoke on the phone yesterday afternoon," Wolf said. "After he explained how supportive you and your family were of having him witness your McGuinness journey as part of his research, I asked him to join the judging delegation as our official documentarian."

"He said what now?" I sat back in my chair. Well, that wasn't exactly how I remembered our meeting going.

Someone cleared their throat, and I looked up to see Ivan standing next to my grandmother. He looked much the same as yesterday—a middle-aged, short, scrawny man wearing faded jeans and a long-sleeved t-shirt that read, 'Eat, Sleep, Write, Repeat.' Fresh nicks and cuts covered his bald head. I wanted to tell him to grow his hair out. Even if he didn't have a lot of it, it would be a far better look. And probably less painful.

"Thanks so much for inviting me to your home, Thea," Ivan said to me.

"Invite you ..." I took a deep breath and tried to channel a sense of etiquette that I didn't really feel. Motioning at an empty chair, I said, "We're delighted to have you. Please have a seat."

"How do you take your coffee?" my grandmother asked Ivan.

Ivan scratched his scalp. "Black, please."

The writer's response got an approving nod from my grandfather. Black was how he believed everyone should take their coffee. It was a sign of a solid and reliable character. Lattes and cappuccinos were frivolous drinks. And don't even get him started on adding ice, whipped cream, or flavorings. Grandpa was even suspicious of the half-and-half my grandmother and I took in our coffee. I could only imagine his horror when he'd first met Hudson and saw him drink coffee more white than brown.

"Take a cookie," my grandmother urged Ivan as she set a cup down in front of him.

"What are they made out of?" Ivan asked.

"The usual," my grandmother replied. "Flour, sugar, and, of course, butter. It wouldn't be a cookie without butter, would it? Almond extract to complement the sliced almonds sprinkled on top."

"Did you say flour?" When Grandma nodded, Ivan frowned. "Sorry, I'm gluten free."

Kayla grinned at Ivan. "Me too."

"Are you as bad at checking food labels as me?" Ivan asked her.

"I'm the worst. Especially when I'm hungry. Or I've had a glass of wine."

As they compared their gluten-free journeys, Wolf interrupted them, saying, "So, where were we?"

"You were telling us how you had invited Ivan to join the McGuinness organization," I said dryly.

Wolf waved a finger back and forth. "Ivan is a temporary contractor, not a permanent employee."

"You're paying me?" Ivan looked hopefully at Wolf.

"Um ..." Wolf squirmed in his seat. "We're paying you in kind."

"'In kind' means what?" Ivan asked.

"Let's discuss the details later." Wolf slapped his hands on the table. "Okay, let's finish up here and head to the barn. We're behind schedule."

"Yes, we should get going," Kayla agreed. "Grace Ryan will be here soon."

My grandmother drew in her breath sharply. "Grace Ryan?"

Wolf furrowed his brow. "Who's Grace Ryan?"

"She's the owner and editor of *The Daily Why*," Kayla said to Wolf. Then she turned to my grandmother. "Of course, you know who she is. It's your local paper."

"I am well aware," Grandma said. "But why is Grace coming here?"

Kayla smiled. "To interview Mr. Olson. This is going to make front page news."

Grandpa shook his head. "Nope."

"What do you mean 'nope'?" Kayla asked.

"Nope," my grandfather repeated.

"My grandfather isn't big on talking," I explained to Kayla. "As you've probably noticed. Interviews aren't really his thing."

"Especially ones with Grace," my grandmother muttered.

"But I'm afraid it's nonnegotiable." Kayla frowned. "Media appearances are at the sole discretion of the McGuinness organization. It was in the contract you signed."

Grandpa pressed his lips together.

Wolf gave Kayla a pointed look. "I don't remember any discussions about the local paper."

"I took care of it," she said breezily. "One less thing on your plate."

"You're my assistant." Wolf glared at Kayla. "But remember, I'm in charge, not you. Got it?"

Kayla looked wounded, and who could blame her? Getting reprimanded in front of strangers, all because you tried to be proactive and help the boss out. Yikes. It's not a fun feeling.

"Tell you what, let's talk about it later. I'm sure we can figure something out," Wolf said in a gentler tone to Kayla. He got up and came round to where my grandfather was sitting and patted him on the shoulder. "Hey, that's a nice hat you've got on there. Wish I had one of those."

"Okay." Grandpa got up and walked over to the coat rack and grabbed a hat from it. "Extra one."

"Cool." Wolf looked at the feed store logo embroidered on the navy blue hat and popped it on his head. "Now we're twins."

I took a step back and cocked my head to one side. The two men were around the same height and build. Put Wolf in a pair of overalls, squint your eyes, and the two of them could look a little bit alike.

Grandma and I hastily cleared the table, and we all headed out the back door. Kayla stopped to look at the garden beds again, chatting amiably with my grandmother while the three men and the two Pomeranians made a beeline for the barn. Once Grandma finished giving Kayla tips about soil temperature, she motioned for us to join the guys.

"Oh, I forgot my phone," I said. "I'll meet you there."

As I headed back out of the house with my phone tucked in my back pocket, I heard someone call my name. "Thea, hold up."

My heart pounded in my chest as I spun around. "Hudson. Is that you?"

"Not just me." He walked toward me, a huge grin on his face, matching my own. "Dr. McCoy is here, too."

Feeling something rubbing against my ankles, I looked down at Hudson's fluffy black and white cat. Kneeling on the ground to scratch the tuxedo's head, I said, "Hello there, Dr. McCoy. Loki and Bjorn will be happy to see you. They missed you while you were in Florida."

"And what about you?" Hudson asked softly. "Did you miss me?"

A wave of anger washed over me, coming out of nowhere. I should be happy to see Hudson after all these weeks, yet ...

"Hey, what's wrong?" Hudson said, helping me to my feet. As he folded me into a gentle hug, I felt my body relax. Yes, I had missed this man. Despite the fact that he had pulled back from me, and not just at the end of our first date, rushing away abruptly. But while he was in Florida with his communication limited to only a few short text messages and a quick impersonal call. And now he wanted to pretend as if nothing had changed?

"Why are you here, Hudson?" I took a few steps back, out of his embrace.

A shadow flicked across his dark brown eyes. "It's Thor's big day tomorrow. You didn't think I would miss it, did you?"

"Oh, I see." I spun on my heel, walking briskly down the garden path. Turning to look over my shoulder, I called coolly. "Come on. He's in the barn."

The look Hudson gave me was a mix of confusion and hurt. I started to relent, but steeled myself. I needed to focus on my grandfather right now, not Hudson. If Wolf gave my grandfather bad news tomorrow about his ball of twine, it would break everyone in my family's hearts. I didn't need Hudson to break mine as well.

***

Hudson tried to pull me aside to talk several times while we were in the barn. I made excuses, busying myself with repositioning the tables and chairs for the dancers' arrival later, assisting Wolf and Kayla with other tasks, and even spent time with Ivan telling him about the history of my family's farm.

After a couple of hours had passed, Wolf declared himself satisfied with the arrangements. "We've got a company delivering some portable stage lights later tonight. Other than that, we're good to go in terms of the set-up. The dancers will be here this afternoon. Can't wait to see them in action." He rubbed his hands together and pointed at my grandfather. "Thor, good news. We canceled Grace Ryan. She won't be interviewing you."

"Or taking pictures, right?" I asked.

Wolf nodded. "Correct."

Kayla folded her arms across her chest. "I'm still not happy with—"

"We'll talk about it later," Wolf said firmly. He turned to the rest of us. "Okay, everyone else, it's time for you to skedaddle. We need to do the preliminary measuring of the ball of twine."

"Are you sure we can't stay?" I asked momentarily wondering if fluttering my eyelashes would help. Thankfully, I resisted that impulse. Sometimes, flirting to get what you want could backfire on you.

I tensed, noticing Hudson had walked up behind me. He was so close I could feel his breath against the back of my neck. I was tempted to lean back against him and feel his arms wrap around me, but I resisted that impulse as well.

"Why is it so secretive?" Hudson asked.

"We need to do a dry run with the measurement equipment," Wolf said. "We wouldn't want to raise any false hopes ... or disappoint anyone unnecessarily."

As Hudson stepped around me, I resisted yet another impulse. But pulling him back toward me would definitely send him mixed messages.

"Measurement equipment?" Hudson asked. "Don't you just use a tape measure?"

Wolf chuckled. "No, siree. Our process is way more thorough than that. That's what makes the McGuinness certification so coveted. When we say something is the world's largest, you can trust that it is. Now, you all scoot. We'll meet you back at the house when we're finished."

Ivan raised his hand. "What about me? As the official documentarian, shouldn't I be present?"

"You can help me set up the lasers," Wolf said. "But after that, you'll have to leave as well. Unfortunately, only permanent employees can be here for the actual measuring."

"How about if you make me a temporary permanent employee?" Ivan suggested.

"Sorry, buddy. No can do."

As my grandparents, Hudson, and I left, Ivan was still trying to cajole Wolf into letting him observe the measuring process. I wondered whether Wolf would cave or not.

When we walked into the kitchen, my grandmother asked what we wanted for lunch. "I have some chicken salad in the fridge. Or I could make grilled cheese and tomato soup. I've been so busy getting ready for the reception, I didn't think about lunch."

"Grandma, you've been slaving over the stove for days now," I said. "Why don't I run into town and get us some pizza? Wolf and the others might want to join as well. I could get enough for everyone."

"Good idea," Hudson said. "I'll come with you."

I shook my head. "No, you stay and keep my grandparents company."

"Good idea," Grandma said. "It's been ages since we've seen you."

Grandpa grunted his approval of this plan.

When I returned with the pizza, Wolf, Kayla, and Ivan were sitting at the kitchen table with the others. After placing the boxes on the counter, I told Kayla and Ivan that I got a gluten-free pizza for them. They did a fist bump.

"Gluten-free buddies," Ivan said.

Kayla grinned. "Gluten-free for life."

While everyone grabbed plates, I asked Wolf, "Have you finished with the measuring?"

"Sure are," Wolf said. "Everything went smoothly."

Ivan broke out in a coughing fit. My grandmother quickly poured him a glass of water. "Sorry about that," he said when he was able to speak again.

Wolf pulled a dark green envelope out of the front pocket of his button-down shirt. He turned it around and showed us the gold wax seal on the back. "See that? That's the official McGuinness logo stamped on there."

I peered at the ornate intertwined 'M' and 'G' pressed into the wax. As I reached out to touch the seal, Wolf yanked the envelope away and tucked it back in his pocket.

"Sorry, young lady. This is confidential." Seeing the crestfallen expression on my face, he gave me a sympathetic look. "It doesn't really matter what it says inside. It's the official measurement tomorrow that counts."

"But how different could they be?" I asked. "You plan on using the same equipment to measure the ball of twine, and you said it worked perfectly."

Wolf shrugged. "We'll see, won't we?"

Before I could press him further, a horn started blaring. We all rushed outside just as a van was pulling up. The driver slid the side door open, and balls of twine poured out, like clowns in a clown car. Not actual balls of twine, but rather people dressed as balls of twine. They were wearing brown leggings and long-sleeved tops, with each of their torsos covered in a large ball made of foam, which had been wrapped in twine.

The costumes couldn't have made for a comfortable ride from Williston, but it was an impressive sight. I could just see the publicity photos now—a human ball of twine eating one of my grandmother's cake pop balls of twine. I was going to have to see if I could get one of their costumes after all this was over. Figuring out what to wear for my grandmother's annual Halloween party? I could check that off my to-do list.

The rest of the afternoon passed quickly while we watched the balls of twine rehearse. By the way they kept bouncing into each other's foam balls, I suspected this was the first time they had practiced in costume. Dr. McCoy and the two dogs didn't make it easy either. Clearly, they wanted to be part of the fun and had to be taken back to the house after a while. Once the dancers had nailed their choreographed steps, they headed back to Williston for the night. Wolf and Kayla also excused themselves. Ivan must have left sometime during the rehearsal without saying goodbye.

I wish I could have said the same for Hudson, but he insisted on a protracted goodbye with my grandparents and me. It was uncomfortable trying to avoid eye contact and knowing that he wanted to speak with me alone. But eventually he got the message and headed back to his place with Dr. McCoy.

My grandparents and I had a light supper and watched the Minnesota Twins game, then we all trundled off to bed before ten. I wasn't in the mood to continue reading my romance novel, opting to drift off to sleep with the help of an Icelandic poetry book I had checked out from the library.

The next morning, I woke up really early after a restless night. No surprise that worrying about how the big day was going to unfold had kept me from sleeping soundly. After a quick shower, I headed down to the kitchen. A dish with a half-eaten piece of toast, an empty coffee cup, and the crumbs by the toaster told me that Grandpa was already up. Since Grandma would have immediately rinsed the dishes and wiped the crumbs off the counter, I knew she must still be in bed.

I was grateful my grandmother was getting a little more shut-eye. It was going to be an exhausting day. Wolf, Kayla, and the rest of their entourage would be arriving at ten to do a final run-through and rehearsal. After a light lunch, Wolf had official photographs and an interview with my grandfather arranged—thankfully not with Grace Ryan.

The guests of honor, including local politicians and the Prairie Dog pageant winner, would show up around half past two for the official measuring ceremony. After that, there was the reception, followed by the clean-up. I was worn out just thinking about it all.

After rubbing my bleary eyes, I reached over to feel the coffee pot. It was cold, so my grandfather had been awake for a couple of hours at least. He'd probably be wanting some more coffee by now. After putting a fresh pot on to brew, I tidied up the kitchen. The sun hadn't come up yet when I headed out the back door with a thermos and some of the leftover almond cookies, but the moonlight allowed me to see where I was going.

"Grandpa, I brought you some coffee," I called out. The barn was dark except for the faint illumination coming from a small portable lamp sitting on the workbench. My grandfather must have been puttering away at something and got up from his stool for some reason. Reaching out to flip the light switch by the doorway, I felt a chill run down my spine. When the lights didn't turn on, my entire body went icy. Something was wrong. I could feel it.

Thrusting the thermos and container of cookies onto a nearby table, I ran around the 'Whymonstrosity,' searching for Grandpa. The lighting was dim, but I could still make out a body clad in overalls and wearing a blue hat sprawled on the floor. I started to rush over to see what had happened, but screeched to a halt when I saw the pair of pruning shears sticking out of his back. A pool of blood surrounded the body. I put my hands to my mouth to keep from screaming. But the scream escaped anyway. How could it not? My grandfather was dead.

CHAPTER 5
GLAZED DONUTS

I stood there, staring at my grandfather's body, unable to move. Why couldn't I move? Why were my feet frozen in place? I had no doubt Grandpa was dead. All those stab wounds and that much blood. He couldn't have survived. No one could. But what if I were wrong? What if he was still clinging to life? I should check and help him and call 911.

Except my feet wouldn't budge. My hands refused to grab my phone from my pocket. My face was stuck in an expression of horror. Why couldn't I move? What was wrong with me?

It's shock, the rational part of my brain whispered to me.

The emotional part of my brain, the same one that loved my grandfather fiercely, whispered something different. It shook me to my core. *If you had brought Edgar to the barn like he asked*, the voice chastised, *this wouldn't have happened. You're the reason he's dead.*

I didn't know how much time had passed since I had walked into the barn and happened upon this terrible scene. It could have been minutes or hours.

"Thor, are you in here?" a familiar voice called out.

My rational brain jostled me. *It's Hudson. Yell! Tell him what happened! Tell him to call the police!*

The advice from my emotional brain was much quieter, and more sinister. *Hide. Don't let him know you're here. He'll blame you for what happened. He'll know you're responsible.*

The two parts of my brain warred with each other for several seconds, for minutes, for hours—I'm not sure. But then Hudson's hands were on my shoulder, and the spell was broken. I could move and speak again.

"Thea, I didn't expect to find you here," he said, his breath tickling my ear. "Where's your grandfather?"

"Grandpa ... he's dead ..." I spluttered, pointing at the body lying next to the giant ball of twine.

Before the words had escaped my mouth, Hudson had already rushed to the body. "Call 911!" he yelled at me.

As I was telling the dispatcher about the situation—the spell immobilizing me having finally broken—Hudson looked up from where he was kneeling and slowly shook his head.

I ended the call, then looked off into the distance. "They're on their way, not that it will make a difference."

Hudson sank back on his heels and groaned. "I can't believe it. Another murder in Why." He shook his head slowly. "Who would have wanted to kill Wolf Shafer?"

It took a moment for the name to register. Hudson had said Wolf, not my grandfather. Grandpa wasn't dead. He was alive! I let out a yelp as happy tears streamed down my face.

Hudson got to his feet, and I started to run over to him. I needed to hug him, to feel a physical connection, to ground myself in his strong arms, to inhale his scent, to—

"Hang on, Thea. Stay where you are," Hudson said as he waved me away. "We don't want to disturb the crime scene any more than it has been already."

My elation vanished. Yes, my grandfather was alive, but Wolf was dead. And not just dead. Murdered. Brutally killed by someone in my grandfather's barn.

Hudson tiptoed cautiously away from Wolf's body, wiping his hands on his pants. He pulled me into his arms and made soothing noises while my tears of joy turned into sobs of disbelief. As horrible as it was to admit, part of my emotional outpouring had to do with another death. The loss of Grandpa's dream. The murder of Wolf meant that

Grandpa's ball of twine wouldn't be formally certified as the world's largest today, if ever.

I knew it was trivial in comparison to the loss of a human life. Still, it was how I felt. After patting Hudson's chest lightly to let him know I was okay, I stepped back and wiped the tears off my face. Touching my face, I grimaced. "Sorry, I think I got snot on your cardigan."

Hudson gave me a gentle smile. "My cardigan is always here for you. You know that."

As I rummaged in the front pocket of my jeans for a tissue that wasn't there, I said, "How am I going to tell my grandfather about this?"

"Here, take this." Hudson held out a handkerchief.

"Who carries handkerchiefs anymore?" I mused, gratefully accepting it from him.

He chuckled. "Nerdy librarians."

"Nerdy looks good on you," I said, falling back into that easy camaraderie we had before Hudson left for Florida. Doubts about his feelings for me flickered through my head, but I batted them away. Things might not have worked out romantically between us, but I knew Hudson was my friend. And right now, I needed a good friend.

"What are you doing here so early, anyway?" I asked as I wiped my nose with the handkerchief.

He gave me a rueful smile. "Dr. McCoy decided to hack up a hairball on top of me while I was sleeping. After I got up to change the sheets, I realized I didn't have any clean ones. I was in such a rush to leave for Florida that I never got around to the laundry. So, why not come here and see if Thor needed any help? I figured he'd be up."

As I was balling up the used handkerchief, I heard someone say, "Thea?"

Looking up, I saw my grandfather standing there, holding a bakery box.

"Alright, Thea?" he asked.

"Sure," I said quickly.

Grandpa looked back and forth between Hudson and me before he said, "Okay."

Hudson held up his hands. "Um, sir, it's not what you think."

"Okay," my grandfather repeated. He held out the box. "Got donuts."

I went to take the box from him, and Grandpa looked past me, finally noticing the body. "What the heck?"

"It's um ..." Hudson cleared his throat. "It's Wolf Shafer. He's dead."

My grandfather's eyes widened as he stepped forward to get a better look. "Dead?"

"Yes," I said softly. "Someone killed him."

"Oh," Grandpa said simply. Then the box fell from his hand, donuts spilling everywhere.

***

"Who contaminated my crime scene?" Chief Jeong demanded.

The chief of police was a short, stocky woman who had been a professional wrestler and served in the Air Force before moving to Why, where she took over the top law enforcement role. My brother had been the acting chief of police for a short time before she arrived. While he had been disappointed not to be chosen for the position permanently, he realized he didn't have the necessary experience.

My grandparents, Hudson, and I had been sitting on a nearby bench when the chief marched up. Grandma was still in her robe and slippers, having been woken up by the sirens approaching the farm. Despite being slightly discomfited by her attire, Grandma refused to leave my grandfather alone and go back into the house to change. She was determined to stay with him until the paramedics and police officers had done their thing, holding my grandfather's hand while we waited. A public display of affection between these two? It showed the seriousness of the situation.

Hudson held up his hand. "Sorry, that was me. I was checking on Wolf to see if he was still alive."

Chief Jeong narrowed her eyes. "I'm talking about the donuts. Who threw donuts all over the crime scene?"

"How do you know they weren't there when Wolf was killed?" I asked.

The chief turned her glare in my direction. Asking questions was her domain, and answering them was what people like me did. "Not that it's any of your business, but the donuts are fresh."

"Yep. Just bought them," Grandpa admitted. When Chief Jeong whipped her eyes in his direction, he added, "They're glazed."

"I don't care what kind they are!" the chief snapped.

"Almost got the sprinkle ones." Grandpa shook his head. "Woulda really messed things up if I did."

Laughter bubbled up inside me as the chief's expression turned to confusion. "I think what my grandfather is trying to say is that if he had gone with the other donuts, then there would be sprinkles all over your crime scene too. Picking them out would have been a nightmare. You should be happy he got the glazed ones."

"Good grief," the chief muttered under her breath. Then she said more clearly, "Listen up, Olsons. Here's what's going to happen—"

"I'm not an Olson," Hudson interjected.

The chief let out an exaggerated sigh as she pointed at me. "Aren't you with this one?"

Hudson squirmed. "Um ... Thea and I are ..."

Taking pity on him, I said firmly, "Hudson is a family friend."

"Not only that," my grandmother interjected. "He's also one of the 'Three Investigators.'"

"What is it with you librarians?" Chief Jeong pressed her lips together. "A man has been murdered, and all you want to talk about are kids' books. Give me a break."

When my grandmother chuckled, a vein bulged on the side of the other woman's head. "Don't be silly, Chief Jeong. Although I have to say I am surprised that you're familiar with the original Three Investigators series. You don't strike me as the type of person who reads, let alone reads children's books."

A vein on the other side of Chief Jeong's head began to bulge. My grandmother and the chief had butted heads during a previous murder investigation. It looked like this one wasn't going to be any different.

Grandma smiled at the chief. "Surely, you remember how Thea, Hudson, and I solved the last murder in this town. We're the 'Three Investigators' I was referring to earlier."

Thankfully, no other veins on the chief's head were bulging. Maybe that's because she was pounding a fist into her hand. It looked painful.

"I think it's more like the 'Three Busybodies.'" Chief Jeong jabbed a finger in my direction. "And you're the worst one of the bunch, Thea. Let me be clear. You—and your fellow busybodies—better keep your noses out of my investigation. Do you hear me?"

Rising to my feet, I squared my shoulders, and jabbed my own finger at the chief. "A man is dead in my grandfather's barn. If you think I'm not going to do everything in my power to find out who the real killer is before you try to pin the murder on my grandpa, then you've got another thing coming."

"Whoa!" Hudson exclaimed.

Chief Jeong went deadly still. Even the veins on her head stopped bulging as a faint smile played on her lips. "And why do you think I would want to charge your grandfather with murder?"

Someone else might have mistaken the tone of her voice for casual friendliness, but I knew better. This was how a predator sounded before it came in for the kill.

I gulped. "I don't. I was just, um …"

"Why are you so worried about your grandfather?" The chief cocked her head to one side. "Is it because you know he's guilty? Why don't you tell me why he killed that poor man? If you're forthcoming now, it will go a long way with the district attorney."

An officer rushed up and whispered something in the chief's ear. She nodded, then stared at each of us in turn. "Don't go anywhere," she warned before spinning on her heel and marching over to the barn.

I sank back down on the bench and put my head in my hands. "I'm so sorry," I said. "I shouldn't have opened my big mouth. Now I've put the spotlight on Grandpa. She probably wasn't even thinking he was connected with the murder until I said something."

"Don't ever apologize for standing up for your family," Hudson said as he patted my back.

"Hudson is right," my grandmother added. "You were trying to protect your grandfather from that horrid woman. I would have done the same thing."

Grandpa reached over and squeezed my hand. I placed my other hand on top of his, noting how cold his skin was.

Turning back to the others, I said, "I'm going to call Leif and give him a heads up."

"Where is he anyway?" Hudson asked. "I would have thought he'd be here already."

"Chief Jeong sent him on a two-week training course," I explained.

"Oh, that's good, right? It's got to beat handing out citations to people who don't scoop up their dog poop. I can't believe the chief had the audacity to call that K-9 duty."

"He's actually on real K-9 duty now," I said. "It happened when you were gone."

Hudson smiled. "That must mean he's on the chief's good side now."

"Uff da," Grandma said. "Chief Jeong still treats Leif like dirt."

"True," I concurred. "But I think Leif has made his peace with it. Besides, he loves working with police dogs. And he's great at it. The sheriff keeps trying to poach him from the Why police department."

"Go call your brother." My grandmother stood and cinched the belt on her robe tighter. "I'm going back to the house while you do that."

Hudson frowned. "But the chief said we had to stay here."

"It's inhumane to make people wait for hours without coffee." Grandma put her hands on her hips. "I'm going to change, and brew a fresh pot. Don't worry, I'll bring some back for the rest of you."

My grandfather gave her a hopeful look.

"Yes, Thor," she said to him. "I'll bring back some cookies, too."

Hudson kept Grandpa company on the bench while I walked over to the troll statue to call my brother. As I waited for Leif to pick up, I rubbed my hand on the troll's belly. The wood in this spot had been worn smooth over the years by all the countless hands of my family, each one of them hoping for good luck.

When I walked out here early this morning, I hadn't stopped to greet Troll. Maybe if I had, things would have been different. Or if I had brought Edgar to visit the barn like the chameleon had requested, things wouldn't have turned out this way. I mentally shook myself. Guilt wouldn't get the target off my grandfather's back. The chief was gunning for him, and it was up to me and the rest of the Three Investigators to find the real culprit.

I was so lost in thought it took me a moment to register Leif's voice in my ear. "Sis, are you there? Did you butt-dial me again? Hello?"

"Sorry," I blurted quickly before he hung up.

"Gotta make it fast," he said. "My break is going to be over soon."

"Long story short," I said. "Someone was murdered in the barn."

Leif was shocked into silence for a moment, then he said, "Um, I'm going to need the long version."

"It was the guy from the McGuinness organization," I explained. "His name is Wolf Shafer."

"Seriously?"

"I found the body a couple of hours ago." A shiver ran through me as I recalled mistaking Wolf for Grandpa. "He was stabbed multiple times with a pair of pruning shears."

"Wow, that's awful," Leif said softly. "Who did it?"

"We don't know. He wasn't from around here, so ..." I swallowed hard, realizing the implications of what I had just said. "It could have been Kayla. She was the only person here who knew him. I should tell Chief Jeong."

"Hang on, Sis. The chief won't react kindly to your butting in and telling her your suspicions. She'll think you're insulting her intelligence."

"No kidding," I said dryly. "We've already had a bit of a run-in."

Leif groaned. "Well, glad I'm not there. She'd be taking it out on me."

"I wish you were here." I paced back and forth. "There's a dead body in the barn. Grandpa's big day has been ruined. He could use your support. We all could."

"You don't think I already feel guilty enough as it is?" Leif snapped. "The training course was scheduled at the same time as the McGuinness event. But it wasn't my decision. You know I wanted to be there when he got the award."

"Sorry. I just miss you, that's all," I said quickly. My voice grew more somber. "I think the chief is going to arrest Grandpa for the murder."

"Why would she do that? You just said that this woman ... what was her name?"

"Kayla Goodwin."

"Okay, Ms. Goodwin was the only person who knew the deceased, right? The chief should put two and two together."

Sitting on the ground underneath an old oak tree, I mumbled, "I guess."

"There's no conceivable reason why Grandpa would have wanted to murder that man. So, no motive."

"But the murder took place in the barn," I pointed out. "Grandpa had means. That's what the chief will say, anyway."

"I think you're overreacting, Thea," Leif said. "Tell you what. I'll check in with one of my buddies on the force to see what's going on. But I know he'll tell me the same thing I'm telling you. There's nothing to worry about."

After we hung up, I walked back toward the bench where we had been sitting earlier, but no one was there. Maybe my grandfather and Hudson had also decided to defy Chief Jeong and walked back to the house to have a cup of coffee inside. Although Leif had told me not to bother the chief with my theory that Kayla murdered Wolf, I decided not to follow his advice. Wrapping up this murder investigation quickly was in the best interest of everybody.

Walking up to the barn, I asked an unfamiliar police officer stationed outside for the chief's whereabouts.

"This is a crime scene, ma'am," he replied. "I have to ask you to clear the area."

"I just need to speak to Chief Jeong for a moment," I said. "It's about the investigation."

"No can do." He pointed back toward the house. "You need to vacate the area immediately."

I folded my arms across my chest. "Don't you care about arresting the killer?"

"Ma'am," he said with a warning tone in his voice. But then his expression softened. "Hey, wait a minute. Aren't you Leif's sister? Man, I'm sorry this happened here. Are your grandparents doing okay?"

After chatting for a few moments and discovering we had a few mutual friends, I asked again where Chief Jeong was.

"She's around the side of the barn, by the gate, talking to a person of interest," he said.

"Phew!" I let out a sigh of relief. "That must be Kayla Goodwin."

He shook his head. "I don't know who they are. I was inside the barn when it started. One of the other guys told me about it."

Making a walking motion with my fingers, I asked, "Is it okay if I poke my head around, and see?"

"Yeah, sure, no problem." I started to walk away when he added, "Hey, do you think I could get your phone number?"

I gave him a rueful smile. "Sorry. I'm seeing someone." It wasn't exactly the truth. But while I didn't know what was going on with Hudson and me, I did know that dating a police officer wasn't something I wanted to do. I worried enough about my brother's safety. A boyfriend on the force, too? That would be too much to cope with. Going out with a librarian was much more appealing. The most dangerous thing that could happen in Hudson's line of work was a paper cut.

As I rounded the barn, my jaw dropped. Chief Jeong was standing next to a squad car with my grandfather. Was Grandpa the 'person of interest' the police officer had been referring to? Had Leif been wrong about the chief? Was she going to arrest him?

Rushing forward and waving my arms in the air, I yelled, "Stop!"

Grandpa stared at me, his eyes blinking slowly.

"You can't arrest him." I thrust my body between my grandfather and the chief. "He didn't do it. I did. I murdered Wolf Shafer."

CHAPTER 6
TORTILLA DOGS

I spent the next several hours in an interview room at the police station. After telling Chief Jeong that I was responsible for Wolf's death, she had put me in the back of the squad car and personally chauffeured me to the station. During the drive, it became clear that the chief never had any intention of arresting my grandfather for the murder. So, I immediately recanted, telling her that the obvious culprit was Kayla.

The chief ignored me. When we arrived at the station, she escorted me to the interview room and left me there to stew on a hard plastic chair. When the police officer, who I had met earlier at the barn, came in to give me a glass of water, he avoided making direct eye contact. I had a feeling he wasn't interested in my phone number anymore.

As the hours ticked by, it became apparent that the chief was just toying with me. No one asked me any questions. It was just me and the bleak interview room with its peeling linoleum floor, dingy white walls, and a faint smell of body odor. Occasionally, I waved at the two-way mirror. But the only person waving back was a tired-looking woman with long blonde hair, blue eyes, and not nearly enough concealer to hide her dark circles. Oh wait, that was me.

Eventually, I summoned the courage to try to open the interview room door. It was unlocked, so I walked out to the front desk and informed the sergeant that I was leaving. He shrugged.

I called Hudson and asked him to pick me up at the station. When I got in the car, my stomach growled loudly, reminding me that I had missed lunch.

"Mind if we grab a bite to eat before you drop me off at home?" I asked.

Hudson grinned at me. "No problem, jailbird."

"I wasn't in jail," I pointed out.

"Close enough," Hudson said. "Did they make you wear an orange jumpsuit?"

I sighed. "Do you think maybe we could save the jokes until I've had some coffee?"

After he pulled into a parking spot in front of Swede's Diner, Hudson squeezed my hand. "Sorry, it's a coping mechanism. I was worried about you."

As his fingers lingered on the back of my hand, I felt my insides melt. My body started to lean toward his when a banging on the car window startled me. Twisting around to see who it was, I spied a very angry woman in her late sixties.

"Hi Grandma," I said after rolling down the window.

She narrowed her eyes as she scolded me. "Confessing to a murder you didn't commit? What were you thinking?"

"How did you know I was here?" I asked meekly.

Hudson cleared his throat. When I turned to look at him, he held up his hands in a 'don't shoot me' gesture.

"Whose side are you on?" I muttered.

My grandmother pointed at the diner. "Inside, young lady. Now."

By the time Norma came over to take our order, Grandma had cooled down. The redheaded waitress snapped her gum as she told us the specials. "We got baked bean pie ... Actually, hang on a minute." Norma turned and yelled in the direction of the kitchen, "Hey, babe. Got any baked bean pie left?"

"Nope. All gone, babe," Swede called back.

"You heard him. No baked bean pie." Norma tapped her pen on her order pad. "What'll it be?"

"What's a tortilla dog?" Hudson asked.

"Exactly how it sounds. A hot dog wrapped in a tortilla," Norma said. "Swede forgot to order buns."

I felt a pang of guilt at the mention of Edgar's favorite food—hot dogs. Had Edgar heard about the murder at the barn yet? I'm sure word had spread all over town by now. People at the library would be buzzing about it. But yet ...

I scanned the diner. No one appeared to be looking in our direction while having whispered conversations. And Norma was the town's biggest gossip. If she hadn't tried to pry any information out of us yet, then maybe things were still under wraps. Though I'm not sure how that was possible. Maybe because all the police action took place on our farm, which is outside of town? Whatever the reason, I didn't really care. As long as I didn't have to field questions about the murder, I was good. It certainly wasn't something I was up for right now.

After Norma finished scribbling down our orders—a chicken salad sandwich for my grandmother, a BLT with extra bacon and tomato for Hudson, and a tortilla dog for me—she lowered her voice. "How's Thor doing?"

"He's fine," my grandmother said. "Why do you ask?"

Norma furrowed her brow. "Because of the 'Whymonstrosity' thing getting canceled. Someone said something about the judge being incapacitated."

Hudson arched an eyebrow. "That's one way of putting it."

I shot him a warning look, and said to Norma, "It's only a minor setback. It'll be rescheduled."

After she bustled off to put our order in, Hudson leaned forward. "Describing death as a 'minor setback' sounds like something you'd read in a Terry Pratchett novel."

"Look, the longer we can keep this thing quiet, the better," I replied. "The minute Grace Ryan gets wind of what happened, she's going to be all over us, demanding interviews for *The Daily Why*."

"You know, I still don't understand why they call it *The Daily Why* when it comes out weekly," Hudson said.

"That's Why for you," I said. "A town of mysteries."

"Well, we have a doozy on our hands," my grandmother said. "The mystery of why Kayla killed Wolf."

"Oh, I know the answer to that," I said. "The two of them were having a relationship outside of work. A romantic one."

"Wasn't Wolf married?" Grandma asked. "I thought I saw a ring on his finger."

I nodded. "He was indeed." After telling them about Wolf and Kayla's conversation—and impromptu make-out session—that I had witnessed at the barn, Hudson let out a low whistle.

"Sounds like Wolf was under some financial pressure," he said.

Grandma shook her head. "Kayla certainly wasn't helping with her demand for a convertible."

"Did you notice the tension between the two of them?" Hudson asked. "Wolf was furious that Kayla had made arrangements with Grace to interview Grandpa."

"They seemed pretty snippy with each other while we were having pizza." I leaned forward. "And that jab of hers about Wolf being old. That was something."

I put a finger on my lip when Norma came over to pour coffee for us. Once she departed, I pulled my cup toward me and blew on it to cool it down. "The best thing that could happen is the police officially announce Wolf's 'minor setback,'" I said, making air quotes, before continuing, "and they also release that they've charged Kayla with the setback. It's a clear-cut case."

After taking a sip of my coffee, I added, "So, let's just relax and enjoy our lunch, okay?"

My tortilla dog was better than I expected, stuffed with melted cheese, sautéed onions and green bell peppers, and chopped tomatoes. Despite being starved, I saved half of it to share with Edgar after we were through here. It was going to be an unpleasant conversation with lots of recriminations about not bringing him to the barn. Maybe some leftover hot dog would help?

As Hudson asked Norma for the check, my phone buzzed. I chewed on my lip as I read the text from Leif.

Slamming my phone on the table, I said, "You're never going to believe this. Kayla has an alibi for last night."

***

After my grandmother absorbed the news that Kayla had an alibi for Wolf's murder, she gave me a sharp look. "Why would Leif text something like that instead of calling? I'll never understand your generation. You have such an aversion to talking on the phone."

"I talk on the phone all the time," I said.

"For work," she pointed out. "When was the last time you called a friend?"

"Well ..."

"Exactly," she said. "I bet when Hudson was away in Florida, the two of you didn't chat on the phone."

I turned to look out the window while I twisted my napkin in my hands. My grandmother was veering onto a subject I didn't want to think about right now. Besides one quick conversation and a few text messages, Hudson and I had barely communicated while he was in the Sunshine State. Now he was back in the fold, sitting at my side like nothing had changed between us. But it had. The shock of finding a dead body in my grandfather's barn had momentarily distracted me from that reality.

After setting my crumpled napkin back on the table, I grabbed my phone. "I'm going outside to call Leif. Be right back."

Fortunately, Leif's training session had finished for the day, so I was able to grill him about his cryptic text message. While he was filling me in on what his buddy on the force had told him about the investigation, I watched Hudson and my grandmother through the window of the diner. They were chatting away, and at one point, Hudson said something that made her laugh. When she reached over and patted his hand affectionately, I gave a wry smile. Hudson was such a good fit with my family.

When I returned back inside the diner and sank into the booth, my grandmother and Hudson looked at me expectantly.

"Well," Grandma prompted. "What did Leif say?"

"Hang on a sec." I grabbed a notebook and a ballpoint pen out of my purse. "I think we should get this down while it's fresh in my mind."

"I like how you think." My grandmother smiled. "Shall we call this meeting of the Three Investigators officially to order?"

Hudson chuckled as he held out his hand. "Want me to do secretarial duties?"

"Sure." I handed him the notebook, but he declined my pen.

"I've got my own." After he pulled a fountain pen out of his messenger bag and uncapped it, he said, "Ready."

"Fancy." Pointing at the blue marbled writing instrument, I asked, "Where did you get it?"

"It's a long story. I'll tell you later." Hudson cracked his knuckles in a comedic fashion, then picked up his pen. "All set."

"Okay, here's the scoop," I said in hushed tones, so we wouldn't be overheard. "Wolf was killed sometime last night between eight and eleven."

"How do they know that?" Grandma asked.

"The police spoke with the guy who delivered the stage lights. According to him, he met Wolf in the barn at seven. It took him about an hour to unload and set everything up."

"So, when the delivery man left at eight, Wolf was still alive and well," Hudson said as he scribbled notes down. "And I assume the coroner determined he had been dead by eleven because of all that stuff coroners do?"

My grandmother chuckled. "Maybe we all need a forensic science immersion course."

"Nah," Hudson said. "I think we can trust what the coroner says without understanding it."

"Totally agree," I said. "And before you ask, the stage light guy isn't under suspicion. They checked him out. He doesn't have any connection to Wolf or the McGuinness organization."

My grandmother nodded. "That seems reasonable. What else did Leif say?"

"The murder weapon was the pruning shears. But we already knew that ..." I took a deep breath, and let it out slowly, trying to banish the image of Wolf's body from my head. "There weren't any fingerprints on it."

"So, the killer had enough presence of mind to wipe the shears clean." Grandma went to take a sip of her coffee, then frowned when she realized her cup was empty. She tried to flag Norma down, but the waitress was busy chatting with Swede through the kitchen door. She sighed, then said, "Go on, dear."

"That's about it," I said. "We have the time of death and the murder weapon, but not much else."

"What about Kayla's alibi?" Hudson asked.

I frowned. "Leif didn't have any details about it. But I suppose it doesn't really matter. The police ruled her out, so that's that."

Hudson tapped his pen on the table. "If not Kayla, then who?"

"I have a feeling we're going to need some dessert while we figure this out." I twisted around in my seat and waved in Norma's direction. She looked over at me, flirted with Swede a few more moments, and finally walked over to our booth.

"Need more coffee?" she asked.

"Uh-huh," I said. "Can we get some pie too, please?"

"Told you already, we're out of baked bean pie." Norma looked at the half-eaten tortilla dog on my plate. "What's wrong? Didn't you like it?"

"No, I'm full." I patted my belly. "But I'll take that to go."

Norma scratched her head. "If you're full, why are you asking about bean pie?"

"No, we want regular pie, dear," my grandmother interjected. She looked over at my plate, and gave me a knowing look. "Even if you can't finish your main course, there's always room for dessert."

"Okay, we got plenty of regular pie." Norma cupped her hand to her mouth and whispered. "It's way better than the bean pie, anyway. I don't know what Swede was thinking when he came up with that recipe. A main dish that also doubles as a dessert? Weird." Then she whipped out her order pad. "Do you want apple or cherry?"

The three of us all opted for apple, making Norma's life easier. After she returned with our pie slices, coffee, and my doggie bag, we sat quietly while we savored our dessert and pondered who could have killed Wolf. Once we had pushed back our plates, I laid out my current theory.

"Wolf was wearing overalls when he was killed," I said. "Plus, a hat from the feed store that Grandpa gave him last night."

Hudson groaned. "Oh no, I get what you're thinking."

"What is she thinking?" My grandmother looked back and forth between the two of us. "Thea, what are you thinking?"

I folded my hands in front of me while I collected my thoughts. Trying to ignore the clenching of my stomach, which I didn't think was due to the tortilla dog and pie, I explained how I had originally believed it was my grandfather who had been killed. "The lighting was pretty dim in the barn," I explained. "And from behind, he looked like Grandpa with the overalls and hat. I didn't expect to find anyone else in the barn at that time of morning. So naturally, I assumed it was him."

"Uff da," my grandmother said. She reached across the table and grabbed my hand. "That must have been awful, thinking your grandfather was dead. It was a good thing Hudson was there for you."

"Yeah, he was the one who figured out it was Wolf," I said.

"He seemed like a nice man," my grandmother said. "Why would anyone have wanted to kill him?"

"You're missing the point," I said slowly. "I think someone wanted to murder Grandpa."

The blood drained from her face. "Thor? No, no, no …"

Now it was my turn to clasp my grandmother's hands in mine. "Don't worry, Grandma. We'll figure out who did it. We won't let them hurt him."

"But who would do such a thing?" She spluttered. "Your grandfather is just a grumpy old man."

I swallowed hard. "Maybe another grumpy old man."

Grandma locked eyes with me, and we both said at the same time, "Denton Watts."

CHAPTER 7
A SPECIAL APPEARANCE BY BUFFORD

The other customers in Swede's Diner continued to chat away to their companions, oblivious to the bombshell I had just dropped on Hudson and my grandmother. The murderer's intended victim had been my grandfather. But due to a horrific case of mistaken identity, Wolf Shafer had been killed instead. Grandma and I realized right away who the culprit was—Denton Watts. Denton had confronted my grandfather in the barn the other day, ordering him to call off the McGuinness event or else. It hadn't been a hollow threat. His unreasonable anger that Grandpa was so close to getting a world record for his ball of twine drove Denton to murder.

It was easy to see how it had happened. From behind, Wolf resembled my grandfather—the same height and build, both wearing overalls and a hat from the feed store. Why Wolf had been wearing overalls, I'm not sure. Maybe he borrowed them from the Larsens' place as some sort of costume? Regardless of how he came to be wearing overalls, it was plausible that Denton had stabbed Wolf in the back with the pruning shears. Wolf had fallen face forward onto the ground. So, when Denton stabbed him multiple times for good measure, he still wouldn't have realized that his victim was Wolf, and not Grandpa.

Squeezing my eyes shut, I tried to recall the crime scene. When I arrived at the barn early this morning ... Wait, what? Had it only been this morning when I discovered Wolf's body? That was less than twelve hours ago. How was that even possible?

"Thea, dear, are you okay?" I heard my grandmother ask.

My eyes flew open. "Sorry. I was thinking about what happened to Wolf and how Denton mistook him for Grandpa."

"Who is this Denton guy?" Hudson asked. "Why would he have wanted to kill Thor?"

"You know, when I first got to the barn, the lights didn't turn on when I flipped the switch," I mused.

"It must have been the fuse," Grandma said. "Your grandfather keeps talking about needing to upgrade the electrical system in the barn."

"Maybe." I looked off into the distance. "The only light was from the moon. The sun hadn't even come up yet. I found Wolf lying on the other side of the ball of twine. I could barely make him out."

Grandma nodded. "Which is why you mistook him for your grandfather."

"Right. But the interesting thing is that the ball of twine would have blocked pretty much any light coming in from the door. I remember a portable lantern on the workbench, though. Hmm ..." I shook my head. "No, I don't think it would have cast any light that far. There had to have been another light source nearby. A very dim one, but enough for me to see Wolf's body."

"You think that's important to the case?" my grandmother asked.

"I'm not sure. I'm probably overthinking things." I rubbed my temples. "Something about it is bugging me. The main lights didn't come on—"

"Could someone please tell me who this Denton fellow is?" Hudson asked again with a trace of impatience in his voice. "I'm not sure that the lighting situation in the barn is the most important thing right now. Aren't you two worried he's going to try again when he finds out it was Wolf he killed and not Thor?"

"Of course!" I snapped and gave Hudson an apologetic look. "Sorry, I know you didn't mean it like that."

"I'm sorry, too," Hudson said gently.

"Right now, there's still plenty of officers at the farm," I said. "As I was leaving the police station, I heard someone say officers would be there until later tonight. But after that ..." Chills ran down my spine as my voice trailed off. What was going to happen if Denton tried to strike again?

I laid out the biggest issue we faced to Hudson and my grandmother. "Earlier today, when I spoke with Chief Jeong, I was adamant that Kayla was the killer. Turns out Kayla has an alibi, so they ruled her out already."

"But that was a perfectly logical assumption," Grandma said. "When we thought the intended victim was Wolf, it made sense to look at the only person in town who knew him and had a reason to want the man dead. Kayla was angry that Wolf hadn't divorced his wife yet. There was a lot of tension between the two of them, both personal and work-related. People kill for a lot less."

"Yeah, I know." I spread out my hands. "But now I'm supposed to show up out of the blue and tell the chief that I have a new theory and suspect? She's not going to take me seriously."

"Look, I'm not Chief Jeong's biggest fan. For some reason, she has a grudge against our family. And sometimes she needs a little help from us when it comes to investigations," my grandmother admitted. "But we still need to respect her professionalism. When we lay out the facts about Denton, the chief will do what's right."

I pressed my lips together. "You're giving her more credit than I would. If she doesn't arrest Denton, I don't know what we're going to do."

Grandma leaned forward, motioning for Hudson and me to do the same. "I'll let you in on a little secret," she said in hushed tones. "Your grandfather isn't at home. On my way over here, I dropped him and the dogs off at your cousin Freya's house. He wanted to get away from the farm. No one else knows he's there."

"That's great," I said. "If need be, the two of you can stay there tonight, safe and sound."

She frowned. "You're not going to stay at the farm by yourself."

"Freya and Josh don't have a lot of room at their place now that they're turning one of their spare rooms into a nursery," I pointed out.

"She can stay with me," Hudson offered. As I felt my face grow warm, he quickly added, "I have a guest room."

"Okay, that's sorted," my grandmother said. "But I don't think it's going to be necessary. Let's pay the check, then go to the police station and talk to Chief Jeong."

"Before we go, can you please give me the scoop on Denton?" Hudson asked. "Pretend it's a dress rehearsal for speaking with the chief."

After explaining that Denton owned the neighboring farm, I told Hudson how there was no love lost between him and my grandfather. "Grandpa got along fine with Denton's dad, Gus. They even helped each other out and occasionally went for a beer together at the lodge. But when Gus got Alzheimer's disease and had to be put into a memory care unit, Denton took over their farm."

"Alzheimer's is the worst," Hudson said. "It's been tough seeing my uncle go through that."

I looked at my grandmother, grateful that she and my grandfather were in good health. Having to support a loved one as they struggled with brain deterioration was rough. It almost made dealing with a murderer on the loose seem like a walk in the park. *Oof.* My thoughts were really turning to a dark place.

Exhaling slowly, I tried to restore my equilibrium. But I gave up. Until Denton was behind bars, I wasn't going to have any peace.

"Anyway," I continued. "That's when things turned ugly. Denton blamed my grandfather for everything. Bad harvest—Grandpa's fault. Fence down—Grandpa again. That sort of thing."

"But none of that was Thor's fault, right?" Hudson asked.

"Of course not. But Denton is the type of person who would rather blame his misfortunes on someone else."

"A large part of it is that the man's jealous of Thor." My grandmother cleared her throat, but started coughing. When her coughing fit persisted, Hudson rushed over to grab a pitcher of water from a nearby table and filled her glass up. She took a few swallows, then gave Hudson a grateful look.

"Thanks," my grandmother said, patting her chest. "I don't know what that was about."

"Too much caffeine." I suggested.

Grandma arched an eyebrow. "Are you saying I should cut back on coffee, dear?"

"Heavens no!" I said with a little laugh. "I know better than that. But maybe have a little more water, okay? You're probably dehydrated."

A slight smile crossed my grandmother's lips. "Dehydrated? Interesting choice of words."

I furrowed my brow, then chuckled. "Oh, I get it."

"Get what?" Hudson asked.

"Denton is a professional dehydrator," Grandma explained.

"Don't you have to make money at something to be considered a professional?" I asked. "I'm not sure Denton turns a profit."

"Good point," she said. "But does it simply boil down to earning money when deciding whether someone is a professional? Take us, for example. The three of us investigate murders, but no one pays us for our work. We're good at what we do, and we deliver results. Does that mean we're any less professional than the detectives on the police force?"

"Pretty sure Chief Jeong would have a different opinion." I chuckled. "Printing up business cards probably shouldn't be on our to-do list anytime soon."

Hudson rapped his knuckles on the table to get our attention. "Mind backing up for a minute? What do you mean by Denton being a 'dehydrator'—professional or otherwise?"

"He dehydrates things," I said.

"Like fruits and vegetables?" Hudson asked.

"Amongst other things." I looked at my grandmother. "Remember when he dehydrated those old tires?"

"Okay, now I know you're joking," Hudson said. "No one dehydrates tires."

"Uh, Denton does."

"You can't fit a tire in a dehydrator. It wouldn't be big enough," Hudson scoffed. "My mom bought one online. It sits on her kitchen counter."

"See, we're back to the professional versus amateur debate. Your mom is an amateur dehydrator. Denton, he's way more serious about it. He built his own custom dehydrators. One of them is almost two stories high. He dehydrates anything he can get his hands on—tires, duffel coats, snowballs—"

"But snowballs are made up of water." Hudson looked perplexed. "There would be nothing left after you dehydrated them."

"I didn't say Denton was bright," I said. "But he is very passionate about extracting moisture from things."

Hudson scratched his head. "Um, that sounds ..."

"Weird?" I suggested.

"Yeah, that's one way of putting it," he said.

I shrugged. "To be fair, is it any weirder than having a giant ball of twine in your barn?"

Hudson jumped to my grandfather's defense. "Absolutely. The 'Whymonstrosity' is quirky, not weird."

"That's sweet, dear," Grandma said to Hudson. "But the line between quirky and weird can be a little blurry at times."

"Denton mostly makes jerky in his dehydrators," I said. "Some of the flavors aren't too bad. But there are some you want to avoid."

"Noted." Hudson nodded. "So why is Denton jealous of Thor?"

"Initially, it was because his farm didn't do as well," I said. "But lately, Denton's been fuming because of all the attention that my grandfather's getting. It was a pretty big deal to have the McGuinness folks come out here. It's all people have been talking about for weeks."

"Killing someone because a ball of twine is getting a lot of publicity?" Hudson pressed his lips together. "That's crazy."

I checked the time on my phone. "We should probably get going."

While Hudson tried to get Norma's attention, my grandmother said, "But that's not the only reason Denton is jealous of Thor."

"Why else would he be jealous?" I asked.

Grandma dug in her purse and pulled out a tin of breath mints. She casually said, "Denton wanted to marry me. When I turned him down, he blamed Thor." After helping herself to a mint, she offered the tin to me. "Your mouth is hanging open, Thea. Looks like you could use one of these, too."

***

After paying the check at Swede's, Hudson, my grand-mother, and I walked outside to make a game plan. While we were discussing what the best approach would be to convince Chief Jeong of Denton's guilt, I felt breath on the back of my neck. Not only was it hot, but it also stank.

I didn't bother to turn around. "Bufford, knock it off."

Bufford snorted in reply.

"Oh, gross! Did you lick my neck?"

Bufford responded with more snorting. Typical. He nudged my back, pushing me forward into Hudson's arms.

Hudson and my grandmother both burst out laughing. I extricated myself from Hudson's embrace, and whipped around to confront Bufford. Shaking my finger at him, I said, "How many times have I told you that my neck is off limits?"

"It's his way of showing how much he likes you," Grandma said.

Bufford stared at me, doing his best to look innocent and adorable. Darn it. How was I supposed to stay mad at him with those mournful dark brown eyes of his? Shaking my head, I reached out and scratched the shaggy fur on his neck.

"You know, we could find another buffalo to be our town mascot if you don't shape up," I whispered in his ear. When Bufford stomped his hoof on the sidewalk, I patted his flank. "I'm teasing. You know that. This place wouldn't be the same without you here."

Reaching into the takeout bag from Swede's, I pulled out some carrots. "These are from Norma."

Bufford made short work of the carrots before he turned to trot down the street in search of other handouts.

Once he was out of sight, Hudson shook his head. "No one back home believed me when I told them about Bufford."

I chuckled. "A buffalo roaming free around town, making friends with everyone, and letting tourists take selfies with him? Yeah, you'd have to see it to believe it."

We chatted for a few more minutes about Bufford, then agreed my grandmother and I should go see the chief while Hudson went home to unpack.

"The three of us together might be too overwhelming," Grandma had pointed out. "Thea definitely needs to be there since she witnessed Denton brandishing a knife and threatening Thor the other day."

"And you need to be there to back me up," I had said to her. "Otherwise, she'll dismiss me out of hand."

Surprisingly, Chief Jeong was fairly receptive when my grandmother and I met with her. She even offered us coffee. After listening to our theory that Denton had killed Wolf thinking he was my grandfather, the chief instructed an officer to bring him in for questioning.

"Questioning? Aren't you going to arrest him?" I asked.

The chief scowled. "Don't push it, Ms. Olson. After we question him, then I'll decide what to do next." Only her expression thawed ever so slightly. "I'll keep you updated."

As we left the police station, I turned to my grandmother. "That settles it. You and Grandpa are going to stay at Freya's until we know for certain that Denton is locked up."

"And you're going to stay at Hudson's place," my grandmother replied, making it sound half like a statement and half like a question.

"Let's figure that out later," I said. "Right now, I need to go to the library."

Looking down at the takeout bag, my grandmother said, "I should have known who the leftover hot dog was for. Doesn't Edgar eat anything else?"

"Flies."

"I guess they're high in protein."

"He's fond of peanut butter cookies, too."

"Oh, I'll have to make him some."

I shook my head. "Don't spoil him."

"He's your guide," Grandma said. "You need to look out for him."

"You realize what a bizarre conversation this is," I said dryly. "We're talking about making treats for a reptile that lives in the library, who only I can see and hear. Of course, I'm grateful I can talk to you about Edgar. You're the only person who could understand."

"It is tricky," my grandmother agreed. "The guides the library bestows on the women in our family have to be kept secret. That's just the way it works."

"Is it?" I furrowed my brow. "Do you really know how this whole thing works? I certainly don't. And to be honest, I'm not sure Edgar does either. The library transported him here and decided to match us up. It's like a horrific blind date that never ends."

"The universe is full of mysteries, dear. They're not all meant to be understood. All you can do is embrace them and learn what you can from them."

I took a deep breath and let it out slowly. "There's something I need to tell you."

"Oh, that sounds serious."

After sitting down on a nearby bench, I filled my grandmother in on Edgar's demand that I take him to the barn.

"Leave the library?" My grandmother's eyes widened. "But I don't think that's possible for a guide."

"Me either," I agreed. "Edgar told me to ask you about a certain bag, one with tapestry on the inside, which would make it possible for me to carry him out of the library."

Grandma looked thoughtful. After a moment, she said, "Oh, I think I know the bag Edgar is talking about. It belonged to your great-grandmother."

"Do you still have it?"

"I haven't seen it in ages. It's probably up in the attic in one of the old trunks." Grandma locked eyes with me. "There's something else you're not telling me."

After a few halting starts, I finally confessed my belief that Wolf would still be alive if I had taken Edgar to the barn when he had asked. "You know how much Edgar annoys me," I said. "So, I blew him off. But if I had done what he asked, then things would have turned out differently."

"Oh, sweetheart, that is absolutely not true," my grandmother said firmly. "Things unfold as they're meant to. You are not responsible for what happened to Wolf."

"But—"

"Guilt is the enemy of intuition," Grandma said softly. "Once you let go of your guilt, you'll be able to hear what your intuition is trying to tell you. And I think what you'll find it's telling you is that Edgar is meant to go with you to the barn to help *solve* Wolf's murder, not to have *prevented* it."

I wrung my hands. "How can you be so sure?"

"Don't forget that I had my own guide. She may not have helped solve murders, but we dealt with our own share of mysteries."

"Ooh, I want to hear about that."

"Maybe another time, dear. Right now, we should get you to the library before Edgar starves to death."

While I went in search of the grumpy chameleon, Grandma perused the new book display. Waving the bag from Swede's back and forth in an enticing manner, I walked through the stacks whispering, "Psst ... Edgar. Got a hot dog here." An older man looking at self-help books shushed me. Giving him an apologetic look, I continued on toward the back of the Collingsworth Wing, where the library housed donated books and magazines for sale.

"That doesn't smell like a nacho dog." Edgar eyed me from a stack of old science fiction paperbacks. He was perched on top of *The Illustrated Man* by Ray Bradbury. That collection of short stories had always stuck with me, in no small part due to the imagery of a man with illustrations on his body. One could see the future in his illustrations, which turned out to be more of a curse than a blessing. It's one of the reasons why I'd never wanted to get a tattoo.

"It's a tortilla dog," I said quietly, so I wouldn't be overheard. "I think you'll like it."

Edgar eyed the bag intently. "Okay, meet me in the break room," he said before doing his trademark whooshing noise and disappearing act.

When I walked into the break room, Edgar was pulling a napkin with his teeth out of the holder onto the table. "Put it there, lady," he said once he had positioned the napkin to his satisfaction.

After I unwrapped the leftovers and set them on Edgar's makeshift plate, I pulled out a chair and took a seat. While he feasted on the tortilla dog, I told him I needed to admit something.

"I didn't take you seriously when you said you wanted to take a field trip to my grandfather's barn."

Edgar swallowed a chunk of tomato, then rotated one of his beady eyes in my direction. "*Quelle surprise,*" he said sarcastically.

"I didn't know you spoke French."

"Don't change the subject."

I held up my hands in surrender. "You're right. Something horrible happened that you need to know about."

"A guy got killed in your grandfather's barn?" Edgar chewed on a piece of tortilla. "I already know that."

"Oh no, people are already talking about it at the library?"

"Yep. Heard someone mention it a few minutes ago."

Pulling my phone out of my purse, I sent a quick text to my grandmother alerting her that the news had broken.

Make sure Grandpa stays at Freya's place where he's safe in case the police don't charge Denton and let him go.

"I need to get going," I told Edgar. "But I want to take you to the barn tomorrow to look at the crime scene. I'm worried the police may have overlooked something. I'll pick you up at nine."

"I'm booked until after one," he said.

"You're booked ... with what?" I asked incredulously. "You're not exactly gainfully employed."

Edgar flicked out his tongue angrily. "I *do* have a job. You. Being your guide is my full-time gig, and let me tell you, the pay and benefits are lousy."

I rolled my eyes. "Okay. Fine. So come with me to do your job tomorrow morning."

"I can't. I'm busy."

"No one else can see or hear you except me. Your social life pretty much consists of hassling me," I said dryly. "You can do exactly that to your heart's content at the barn tomorrow first thing."

"Just because I'm invisible, doesn't mean I don't have a social life or things to do, lady," Edgar grumbled. "Not that it's any of your business, but the staff meeting is at ten tomorrow. Then there's a birthday thing for one of the library assistants at noon. One of the gals is going to make cheesecake. No way am I going to miss that."

"Seriously? Last time I checked, you weren't a member of the library staff."

"I am the official Senior Library Guide and Guardian," Edgar announced pompously. "That alone automatically makes me a member of staff. I need to know what's happening around the joint, and to do that I go to the meetings. I'm not sure why that's so hard to get through your thick skull."

"What do you mean by 'senior?' How old are you exactly?"

"Hey dummy, focus. Pick me up tomorrow at two pm. Bring the tapestry bag. Got it?"

I nodded as I scooped up the mess Edgar had left on the table.

"Oh hey, there's something else you need to do before tomorrow." Edgar belched, then rubbed his chest with his little hand. "Darn onions. Anyway, go back to the stacks where the used books are for sale and pick up *The Mystery of Monster Mountain*. Read it before tomorrow afternoon."

After tossing the trash in the garbage can, I called over my shoulder, "Nope. No way. I don't have time for another one of your stupid book club meetings."

"It's a Three Investigators book, lady," Edgar said. "And it'll help you crack this case."

"I already know who did it—Denton Watts."

Edgar flicked his tongue in and out. "Maybe. Or maybe not."

CHAPTER 8
A PICKLE EMERGENCY

I was dimly aware of a man's voice asking, "Thea, Thea, are you okay?" They sounded like Hudson, but he was in Florida. I could picture him in my mind, emerging from the ocean wearing a wetsuit and holding a surfboard. As he started to walk up the beach, a giant ball of twine barreled toward him, knocking him into the sand and crushing him. Screaming, I rushed toward him. I needed to save Hudson before it was too late. But when I reached him, I realized he wasn't wearing a wetsuit. He was wearing overalls, and it wasn't Hudson after all. My grandfather was lying there unconscious ... or was he dead? Anxiety bubbled up inside me—a giant ball of twine attacked my grandfather. Who would its next victim be?

"Thea, wake up. You're having a nightmare." The man's gentle voice filtered through my consciousness. Suddenly, I felt a gentle pressure on my chest, followed by a plaintive meow.

A meow? Grandpa didn't make meowing sounds. What was going on? The scene changed in my mind. Now, a fluffy black and white cat played with the ball of twine, batting at it and creating a tangled mess. There was a gentle pressure on my cheek and a more insistent meow this time. My eyes fluttered open, and I was greeted by the sight of Dr. McCoy sitting on top of me. He gave me several slow blinks before batting my nose with his paw.

"Dr. McCoy, what are you doing here?" I mumbled, confused as to why Hudson's cat was in my bedroom. Feeling groggy, I tried to sit up in bed, and quickly realized two things. First, I wasn't at home. Second, cats get to decide when a human moves, not the other way around.

While the tuxedo cat nestled into my chest, purring loudly, I resigned myself to lying back down on Hudson's couch. I was snuggled under a blanket in his living room with sunlight streaming through the window. Had I fallen asleep here the previous evening? The last thing I remembered was arriving at Hudson's place late at night, utterly exhausted.

The extreme fatigue was totally understandable. Up before dawn yesterday, I had gone to the barn and discovered Wolf Shafer dead next to the 'Whymonstrosity.' Then Hudson, my grandparents, and I had sat around for hours while the police secured the crime scene and began their investigation. Fearing Chief Jeong was going to arrest my grandfather for murder, I had foolishly confessed to killing Wolf. Cue another several hours hanging out at the police station before realizing the chief was toying with me and never planned on filing charges.

An impromptu Three Investigators meeting at Swede's Diner followed. Finding out Kayla had an alibi and couldn't have killed Wolf led us to the shocking realization that my grandfather had been the intended victim all along. Turns out Denton Watts was the killer. The police took him in for questioning, but we weren't sure if they would charge Denton right away. So, my grandparents stayed at my cousin's house instead of the farm in case he tried to strike again.

From there, I went off to the library to chat with Edgar. He'd made such a mess in the break room devouring my leftover tortilla dog while we talked. Seriously, tomato and cheese were all over the floor by the time he was done. The tiny reptile might be invisible to everyone but me, but his food scraps certainly weren't. Of course, I was the one who cleaned everything up while Edgar watched. He didn't care if the library staff thought I was a pig. After he bossed me around some more, he said, "Get the tapestry bag and pick me up tomorrow afternoon, lady." So, I went off in search of the bag.

It was after seven when I arrived at the farm. The police were no longer on the premises. Though when I walked out to the barn, crime scene tape was still attached to the building. Worried for my own safety and being alone on the property, I called Leif. He assured me that Denton was still being held at the police station. If he were released, Leif would alert me and my grandparents right away.

When I walked into the house, a silent eeriness greeted me. No dogs rushed up to welcome me, yipping with excitement and wagging their tails. My grandmother wasn't bustling around the kitchen. And my grandfather wasn't watching baseball in the other room. It was just me. Was this what living alone was going to be like?

I quickly gathered clothes and toiletries in overnight bags for my grandparents and myself, then went up to the attic to search for the tapestry bag. It took a couple of hours to find it, in part because I kept stopping to look at the various treasures and memories I stumbled upon—the dollhouse my grandfather made for me, Leif's scouting badges, carved antique wooden butter molds, and my parents' wedding album among other things.

The tapestry bag finally turned up in a dusty rose-colored antique trunk at the back of the attic. I paused to admire the traditional decorative Norwegian rosemaling. Someone in my family must have painted the blue, gold, and green scrolls and floral designs which had transformed this plain trunk into a work of art. Once things got back to normal, I'd have to ask my grandparents about it. Maybe I might even try my hand at rosemaling. Lately, it seemed like my only hobby was solving murders. I could probably do with a more relaxing pastime.

I opened the lid and discovered the tapestry bag lying at the bottom of the trunk underneath some woven tablecloths. Sitting back on my heels, I admired the bag. It was exquisite, made of a supple dark brown leather hand stamped with an intricate celestial pattern. The interior was lined with a tapestry that would make any bibliophile scream with delight—books, sheets of paper, and writing instruments all woven into the fabric in rich jewel tones.

How was it that I had never seen this bag before? *Because you never had a need for it until now*, a small voice whispered. Whipping my head around, I searched in vain for the speaker. Goosebumps prickled my skin as I realized that there wasn't anyone in the attic with me. At least not anyone human.

Wrapping my arms around myself, I thought back to my time living in Minneapolis working for a big company. My life in the big city certainly had its excitement—a fast-paced corporate work environment, nights out on the town, and a major baseball team, among other things.

When I moved back to Why, I knew I would be trading that in for a quieter life and more time with my family. But what I hadn't counted on was discovering a mysterious hidden world full of guides and disembodied voices in this part of North Dakota. It could be pretty disconcerting at times. This was definitely one of them. Shivers ran down my spine. I needed to get out of here.

Quickly gathering up the tapestry bag, I grabbed the overnight bags I had packed earlier, dashed out to my car, and raced to my cousin's house. When I walked inside, it felt warm, cozy, and safe. Bjorn and Loki, along with my cousin's massive Bernese Mountain dog, greeted me with excited barking. Grandma and Freya were in the kitchen baking cookies while Grandpa and my cousin's husband, Josh, sat in the family room with the game on.

Freya made me a sandwich, then showed me what they had done to get the nursery ready so far. There were still some finishing touches Freya and Josh wanted to add. Though they had plenty of time to get everything done since the baby wasn't due for another two months. After telling her about the antique toys I had seen in the attic, which might look cute in the nursery, I said my goodbyes and headed to Hudson's to spend the night.

"You okay, Thea?" Hudson asked, interrupting my thoughts. He was perched on the coffee table, holding a mug in his hand that had a definition of a librarian on it that read 'keeper of books, guardian of knowledge, professional shusher.'

"Yeah, sorry." I rubbed my eyes. "So much has happened in the past twenty-four hours. I feel completely out of sorts. I had this awful nightmare. Have you ever seen that old British show *The Prisoner*?"

Hudson shook his head. "I don't think so."

"Leif and I watched it a few years ago." I brushed my mouth with my hand, trying to get Dr. McCoy's fur off my lips. "It was pretty strange. A secret agent is abducted and wakes up in a mysterious village. There was this large, menacing white ball that would attack people if they tried to escape."

"Hmm, that does sound weird. That's what you were dreaming about?"

"Not exactly. First you were surfing—"

"Oh, you were dreaming about me." Hudson grinned, but then his smile faded. "Wait a minute. You were having a nightmare about me?"

Turning my head to the side so I could see Hudson better, I said in a reassuring tone, "No, it wasn't like that."

After explaining that my dream was about an evil ball of twine and probably related to my fears for my grandfather, Hudson set his mug down on the coffee table. He scooped the cat off me. "I think you need some coffee. And this little guy probably wants some more crunchy nuggets."

By the time I freshened up and returned to the living room, Hudson had a large latte and a blueberry muffin waiting for me. The aroma of the coffee was heavenly. Tea drinkers were a mystery to me. Why would anyone want to start their morning without the tantalizing smell of roasted coffee beans filling the air?

"I had the guest room all set up for you," Hudson said as he handed me my coffee drink. "But you fell asleep on the couch five seconds after you sat down. I didn't have the heart to wake you up."

I patted the couch. "No problem. This was pretty comfy. And thanks for putting a blanket over me."

"I had been hoping to talk with you last night before you conked out." Hudson sat at the opposite end of the couch and twisted his body to face me. "We really need to talk, Thea. Things have been different between us since I came back."

Grabbing one of the throw pillows, I clutched it to my chest and folded my legs underneath me. "Yep, it has been different." I took a deep breath, then let it out slowly. Fixing my gaze on Hudson, I blurted out, "What happened? I thought there was something between us, but the minute you left for Florida it was like you became a stranger."

Hudson gulped. "I'm sorry," he eventually said. "I could tell you it's because I was so busy dealing with family stuff. My uncle was deteriorating fast, what with his dementia and other health issues. My aunt wasn't coping well with being his caregiver. The two of them don't have kids, and while the rest of the family pitched in, my aunt really needed someone to help out full time while she sold the house and moved my uncle into a memory care unit. So, I volunteered—"

"Oh no, I'm sorry," I interjected, feeling awful for what he and his family were going through. "That's a lot to deal with. You're a good nephew to help them out."

"You didn't let me finish," Hudson said. "It was tough, and I was busy helping out, but that's not the reason why I kept my distance from you."

"I wasn't sure if you realized you had pulled away."

"I definitely know I did." Hudson chewed on his bottom lip for a moment before he said, "Being in Florida, it was easy to pretend that all of this didn't exist. My job as Why's library director, the friends I've made here, this house I'm renting ..." Hudson's voice trailed off as he stared down at the floor. He let out a long sigh, then looked back at me. "It was easy to pretend the feelings I have for you weren't real. But the minute I saw you again in your grandmother's garden, it was like that quote from *Anna*

Karenina 'He could not be mistaken. There were no other eyes like those in the world. There was only one creature in the world who could concentrate for him all the brightness and meaning of life. It was she.'"

A lump formed in my throat. My eyes watered. Was it possible Hudson really did have romantic feelings for me? Doubt bubbled up inside me. This man sitting across from me had suffered a great tragedy in his past, losing both his wife and unborn child. Although he had told me previously that he was ready for another relationship, once Hudson returned home to Florida and placed a physical distance between us, things had changed. Maybe it had been a sign, and it wasn't the right time for him and me.

But before I could share my fears with Hudson, there was an urgent phone call from my grandmother. "Thea, you have to get to the Little Pickle immediately," she said. "It's an emergency. I'll meet you there. Hurry!"

***

Bursting through the sliding glass doors of the Little Pickle, I dodged shoppers and their grocery carts. I only skidded to a stop when I saw my grandmother laughing about something with one of the cashiers, Ingrid Ragnhild. Clearly, the emergency Grandma had me rush to the

Little Pickle to help deal with had been resolved, otherwise the two of them wouldn't be giggling like a couple of schoolgirls.

Ingrid had been a fixture at the Little Pickle for as long as I could remember. She was a stunning woman in her mid-fifties—high cheekbones, green eyes, and long blonde hair worn in heavy braids twisted around her head in a style that wouldn't look out of place at the annual Scandinavian festival. Only Ingrid could manage to make the green pickle print apron that all the cashiers had to wear look stylish.

"Oh, there you are, dear." My grandmother waved me over. "Ingrid was just telling me the funniest story about the rehearsal last night."

"At the community theater?" I asked.

"That's right. Ingrid is the leading lady in their production of *The Music Man*," Grandma explained. "It's one of my favorite musicals. I can't help tapping my toes when they sing 'Seventy-Six Trombones.' Although sometimes I think Harold Hill got off rather lightly in the story. Imagine trying to con an entire town and still getting the girl?"

"At least Harold Hill was redeemable in the end. Not like some con men I could mention," Ingrid said bitterly.

"Oh, you must be talking about those guys who were going around trying to sell premium gutter systems," my grandmother said. "They bilked a bunch of folks out of thousands of dollars, then skipped town last week without ever installing anything."

Anger flashed in Ingrid's eyes, making me wonder if she had fallen victim to the same fraudulent salesmen. After a moment, she adopted a blander expression. "Exactly. Those guys should be shot."

"Not literally, of course," I said with a smile.

Ingrid waved a hand in the air. "No, of course not. But they should be arrested and prosecuted. Not that the police care. They'll do nothing about it and still demand that we pay higher taxes, so that they can buy new squad cars."

As my grandmother and I exchanged looks, Ingrid quickly added, "I don't mean Leif. I'm sure he's a good officer. It's the chief of police I'm talking about."

I felt conflicted. On one hand, Chief Jeong was a real pain in the you know what, and she hadn't treated my brother well. However, I didn't doubt her commitment to public safety. Sometimes she did need to be pointed in the right direction though, like yesterday when Grandma and I laid out the case against Denton. But overall, she did a decent job with run-of-the-mill police work.

Before I could figure out how to respond, a customer came over and asked Ingrid where the smoked oysters were located. "Don't forget to get tickets to *The Music Man,*"

Ingrid called over her shoulder as she went to help the customer.

Turning to my grandmother, I asked, "What was this big emergency?"

"Your grandfather wants pickles," she explained.

"Grandpa wants pickles?" I arched an eyebrow. "That's why you called me in a panic and told me to get down here ASAP?"

"I wasn't panicking."

"Hmm, right. A craving for pickles is hardly an emergency, though."

"Well, he was very insistent about it. We looked in the fridge, but Josh and Freya are completely out of pickles."

"I'm surprised you didn't check the cupboards for a backup jar," I said dryly.

"Oh, we did. Found some peanut butter there. It'll keep Thor occupied for a while, but peanut butter isn't really a good substitute for pickles."

I furrowed my brow. "Okay, I'm confused. When did Grandpa become such a pickle fiend?"

"It started around three this morning."

"Right," I said slowly. "So, this is a relatively recent obsession with pickles."

"Pickled vegetables actually have a lot of health benefits," Grandma pointed out. "They're a good source of antioxidants, not to mention vitamins K and C."

"Um, okay."

"Pickles can also help relieve stress," she added.

"Uh, you might be thinking about pickleball," I said. "Exercise is good for stress reduction. Dill pickles, maybe not so much."

"He actually wants the bread-and-butter kind."

"What's really going on?" I asked.

My grandmother fiddled with the paper bags at the end of the checkout counter for a moment before she said, "Thor's sudden craving for pickles is probably his way of avoiding thinking about what happened yesterday. If pickles can help him forget that someone was murdered in his barn, then buying pickles is an emergency."

I nodded. "You're right. Let's get the man some pickles."

As we walked over to the aisle where the pickles, salad dressings, and condiments were located, my grandmother apologized, "I shouldn't have asked you to rush over here. But I'm glad you did. It's nice to have your company. To be honest, your grandfather was driving me a bit batty this morning. And since we don't want him to show his face in public until we know Denton is behind bars for sure, it was a good chance for me to get out of the house for a bit."

While Grandma was trying to decide between two different brands of pickles, I wandered over to the coffee aisle. Hudson had been sweet to let me crash at his place. Maybe I should bring him a few bags of gourmet coffee as a thank you. A couple of employees were restocking the shelves, so I waited for them to finish. After they moved their cart out of the way, I could get to the coffee section.

One of the employees was griping about Ingrid. "She's refusing to do deliveries today," the young woman complained.

"But she's on the schedule all week for deliveries," her male colleague replied.

"You know what Ingrid is like," the woman said. "She flirts her way out of anything she doesn't want to do. Bats her eyelashes at the manager and poof, she doesn't have to do deliveries anymore."

"Wait, that doesn't make sense," the man said while placing boxes of cereal on the shelf. "She was really eager to do that delivery last night when her shift ended."

The woman shrugged. "Probably because it was out of town and paid extra. But maybe they were lousy tippers."

"She acts like she's so high and mighty," he grumbled. "Just because she was in one commercial a million years ago, doesn't mean she's special. Ingrid should do deliveries, the same as us. Being a failed Hollywood actress shouldn't be a get out of jail free card."

"Exactly." The woman gave him a thumbs up, then caught sight of me. "Oh, sorry, didn't see you there. Here, let me get that out of your way," she said as she pushed the cart to the side of the aisle.

While I picked out some coffee for Hudson, I smiled to myself. Norma, the waitress at Swede's, would have killed to hear gossip like this. As the queen of the town's rumor mill, she believed people should only spill the beans in her presence at the diner.

My grandmother and I checked out—pickles and dog chews for her, coffee and cat treats for me—and we parted ways. With a few hours to kill before I was due to pick up Edgar at the library, I went back to Hudson's place to do some work. He would have already left for the library, so there wasn't any fear that we'd have to finish our soul-bearing conversation. To be honest, I needed some time to myself to absorb what he had said earlier. It had been a lot.

A few spreadsheets and project plans later, not to mention some snuggles with Dr. McCoy, I closed my laptop and grabbed the tapestry bag. When I walked into the library, Hudson was busy explaining some of the children's programs to a patron. I gave him an awkward wave and headed back to the break room to try to locate Edgar. One of the library assistants was in there and offered me some leftover cheesecake. It was hard to resist. But, because I wanted to get this field trip with Edgar over with as quickly as possible, I politely declined.

"Where is he?" I murmured to myself as I roamed the stacks. Edgar had specified a two pm departure. I was here on time. Where the heck was he? It wasn't until I was standing by the shelves with the books for sale that I heard Edgar's calling card, 'The Whoosh.'

Geez. When did I start mentally referring to it as 'The Whoosh?' It's not like his mystical transportation system was trademarked or anything. It's a 'whoosh,' plain and simple. Well, it's not all that easy—moving a chameleon around through time and space was probably pretty complicated from a physics standpoint. But I couldn't think about that now, or ever, really. Physics made my brain hurt.

Edgar thumped his tail on the stack of books he was perched on. "Why is this still here, lady?"

"Why is what still here?" I replied.

"*The Mystery of Monster Mountain,*" he said. "I told you to buy it, remember?"

"You have got to be kidding me." I put my hands on my hips. "Do you have any idea what my day was like yesterday? I didn't have time to read a book."

"Your grandmother would be so disappointed if she heard what you just said. The granddaughter of a librarian doesn't have time to read? What an embarrassment you are to your family."

I scowled. "What could you possibly know about families?"

"A lot," Edgard snapped with an edge, his tone even more sharp than usual.

"Wait a minute, do chameleons have families?" I asked slowly.

"Stop changing the subject, lady," he snapped. "Buy the dang book."

"Let's get this field trip over with." I unlatched the tapestry bag and held it up to the shelf. "Get inside."

Edgar refused to budge. "Buy the book first."

"Get in the bag."

"The book."

"The bag."

This back and forth continued until I spotted a man in a wheelchair headed in our direction. He said hello to me, then looked at the books for sale. "Hey, could you hand me that one—*The Mystery of Monster Mountain*? It's underneath that purple book," he asked, pointing it out. "My son loves the Three Investigators. I should get that for him."

Edgar let out a low growl, which intensified as I reached for the *Monster Mountain* book. "If you give the book to that guy, you'll regret it for the rest of your life."

My natural reaction was to scoff at his threat and hand the book in question over, but my gut told me to take Edgar's warning seriously.

"Sorry," I apologized to the man. "Someone already claimed this book. I was getting it for them."

It wasn't really a lie—Edgar had claimed the book for me. Fortunately, the man didn't seem that bothered, telling me his son would be just as happy with the Nancy Drew book on the bottom shelf.

After he wheeled away with *The Secret of the Wooden Lady* in his lap, Edgar told me to put the Three Investigators book in the tapestry bag. "You can pay for it later." He hopped in, landing on top of the book. "Come on, let's get going." As I was latching the bag, he added, "You can tell me all about your little sleepover with Hudson on the way to the farm. He was pretty distracted at the staff meeting this morning, and I want to know why."

CHAPTER 9
IT'S ABDUCTION, DUMMY!

"Lady, open this thing! I'm suffocating in here," Edgar griped and moaned as I pulled up in front of my grandparents' farmhouse.

Ignoring his complaining, I got out of the car and slung the tapestry bag over my shoulder.

"Stop jostling the bag!" he cried out. "Are you trying to break my bones or what?"

"Calm down already." After placing the bag on the trunk of the car, I opened it and Edgar hopped out. "It was your idea to come to the farm," I reminded him. "Remember? You insisted on a two o'clock departure. Honestly, I'd think you should be happy that this magical bag trick worked. Look around you. You're out of the library on a grand adventure."

"So?" The annoying reptile rolled his eyes. "By the way, you're a really bad driver, lady."

"How would you know? You were inside the bag the whole time."

Edgar flicked out his tongue angrily. "And whose idea was that? I wanted to see the countryside."

Actually, it was my idea. The thought of Edgar perched on the dashboard doing the backseat driver thing did not sound appealing to me in the least. Leaving him in the bag seemed like a much better option. Of course, he let out a stream of complaints during the entire drive, so maybe it had been a bad call on my part.

"Bend down a little, blondie," Edgar ordered.

"Huh?"

"What, are you deaf? Bend down."

I eyed him suspiciously. "Why do you want me to bend down?"

"So, I can get on your shoulder. Duh! No way am I riding in that bag while you walk to the barn from here." Edgar hopped back and forth on the trunk. "Come on already, lady. Bend down already. They're showing *National Treasure* at the library tonight, and I want to be back in time for it."

"Ooh. That is a good movie. Maybe I should stay and watch it, too." I crouched down, and Edgar hopped onto my shoulder. "You remind me of a pirate's parrot sitting up there."

I burst out laughing when Edgar replied, "Aye, matey."

"Sometimes you're alright, little guy," I admitted.

Edgar flicked his tongue out, narrowly missing my cheek. "Don't call me that."

"What, you mean 'little guy'?" I asked. "Your name is Edgar, so I made an assumption about the guy thing. I suppose I should have asked first."

"The 'guy' part is fine," he snapped.

"Ah, now we're getting to the heart of the matter. You object to being called 'little.' But come on, you are a little itty-bitty thing." I gestured with my hands as though I were measuring something. "You can't be more than eight, maybe nine inches tops."

"Eleven and a half, lady!" he yelled. "I'm eleven and a half inches long."

There was a definite downside to letting Edgar ride on my shoulder—the proximity to my ear. Turns out tiny reptiles have powerful lungs, and when they scream in your ear, watch out!

"Tell you what, why don't we round up and call it a foot." I grinned. "You know, like a foot-long dog."

"Why do you have to talk about hot dogs at a time like this?" Edgar whined. Thankfully, his whining volume was much quieter, sparing my eardrums from more pain. "I'm starving."

"How can you be starving? You had cheesecake earlier today at the library. There are a lot of calories in that dessert. It should keep you going for hours."

"It wasn't a New York style cheesecake. The woman who made it used ricotta cheese instead of cream cheese." Edgar shuddered. "Yuck, I couldn't eat it."

"Ricotta." I grinned. "What a heretic."

As we walked toward the barn, Edgar took in the surroundings. He appeared particularly fascinated with the troll statue. "Maybe we should read *The Sea of Trolls* for one of our future book club meetings?"

"Please, no more homework," I said. "I already have a stolen book in this bag to read."

"It's only stolen until you pay for it," Edgar stated sagely.

Considering I had an unpaid-for book on my person, debating Edgar's dubious ethics didn't seem advisable. As we neared the barn, I was confronted with another ethical dilemma. Since this was my grandparents' property, did the yellow crime scene tape really apply to me?

As if reading my mind, Edgar said, "It's just tape, lady. It can't tell you what to do."

Carefully twisting and turning my body to avoid tearing the tape, I slipped through the barn door. I flicked on the lights, then said, "Darn it. They're still not working. How are we supposed to see in here? Hey, you don't happen to have X-ray vision, do you?"

"X-ray vision means you can see through things, dummy. I think you mean infrared vision."

"No, I didn't, *dummy*," I said, throwing his favorite insult back at him. "I meant night vision."

"Night vision is a type of infrared vision, *dum-dum*." Edgar swatted my cheek with his foot. Honestly, that kind of behavior was so much more endearing when done by a cute, fluffy, black and white cat than by an obnoxious chameleon. "Grab that flashlight over there," he ordered.

"Where?" I looked around in the dim light trying to spot it.

"On top of that hay bale," Edgar said.

The flashlight helped a bit, but it was still hard to make out much as we wandered around the barn. The stage lights that had been delivered the night Wolf was killed were standing near the door, presumably ready to be picked up by the rental company. But they wouldn't do me much good without a generator to plug them into. When the police had been here, they had slid open the larger barn doors to let light in. Only I couldn't do that without disturbing the caution tape the police had plastered on them.

I walked around the giant ball of twine, being careful to sidestep the spot where I had discovered Wolf lying in a pool of blood.

"Whoa, hold up!" Edgar exclaimed. "Look at that there."

After aiming the flashlight at the spot Edgar indicated, I gasped. "Someone cut the twine."

A section of the 'Whymonstrosity' had been slashed, presumably with a knife. Once the severed strands of twine were removed, the ball's circumference would be significantly reduced, perhaps no longer even world record sized.

"This was deliberate," I said.

"Impressive deduction," Edgar quipped sarcastically.

"I think you mean abduction, *dummy*."

Edgar snorted. "You think aliens had something to do with this?"

"I wish they would abduct you," I muttered under my breath. "No, I'm talking about abductive reasoning. You start with an observation, like the severed strands of twine here. Then, you find the simplest and most reasonable explanation. In this case, it was deliberate destruction by someone. Someone who didn't want Grandpa to get the world record. And we all know who that was—Denton."

I stood back to get a better look at the cut marks before adding, "Abductive reasoning is what Sherlock Holmes used when solving cases. People often get it confused with deductive reasoning."

"Lady, you are no Sherlock Holmes."

"Nor would I want to be. Arrogance and a complete lack of empathy aren't qualities I want to emulate." I turned my head and looked at Edgar. "He sounds more like your role model."

"Well, I do like his hat. Don't you think something like that would look good on me?"

"Let's table the fashion discussion until later, okay?"

After a thorough examination of the barn, which didn't turn up much else of interest, Edgar asked if we could have a look outside. We made a circle around the exterior of the building looking for any clues the police might have missed, but came up short there as well.

"I think this trip was a bust," I said.

"No, we still need to look over there." Edgar gestured at something in the distance.

"Where? You mean the gate?"

Edgar bobbed his head up and down, then told me to pick up the pace.

Naturally, I slowed down my pace. As we leisurely strolled over to the gate, I explained that it was the only vehicular access point to the barn.

"We already know that the guy delivering the stage lights drove through it the night Wolf was killed. He left at eight, which means ..." I stopped in my tracks and thought for a moment. "Hey, that's something we need to check on. Who unlocked the gate to let the delivery guy in? Also, was the gate locked after he left? If so, that meant Denton would have had to climb over the gate to get to the barn."

"Couldn't he have come the way we did?" Edgar asked.

"No," I said. "If he had parked his truck at our place and taken the garden path to get back here, the dogs would have alerted us. Anytime there's someone outside, they start barking like crazy."

"Are you going to stand here all day, lady?" Edgar stamped his feet against my shoulder like a miniature jockey spurring a horse on.

"Knock it off, or it's back in the bag for you," I said firmly.

When we reached the gate, Edgar hopped onto the top rail. Skittering over to the end, he motioned at the barbed wire fence connected to the gate. "Something's snagged there."

Being careful not to get my foot caught in the cattle guard that served as a barrier to prevent livestock from getting through the gate—their hooves couldn't walk across the metal bars to escape. I took a photo of the scrap of fabric with my phone, then used a tissue to gently pull it off the barbed wire.

"It looks like denim," I said, holding it up for Edgar to see. "What do you want to bet Denton has a hole in his overalls exactly the same shape as this piece of fabric?"

"Got an evidence bag on you, lady?" When I shook my head, Edgar suggested I keep a stock of them on hand for future cases.

"How did the police miss this?" I mused. After carefully wrapping the denim fabric in the tissue to protect it, I placed it in the tapestry bag for safekeeping. "It supports the case against Denton. He climbed over the gate to get to the barn, snagging his overalls in the process. After sneaking inside, he must have started to slash the twine with his knife. But he heard someone on the other side of the ball and became desperate—worried he would be caught vandalizing the 'Whymonstrosity.' So, he rushed over and stabbed him in the back."

"A good theory, but there is one tiny problem with it."

I frowned. "What's that?"

"Wolf was killed with pruning shears, not a knife."

"Um ..." I waved a hand in the air. "Details. We can figure that part out later. What's important is that we have proof Denton climbed over the gate. We need to get this fabric to the police. They can search his house for the incriminating overalls. Let's just hope he hasn't tried to dehydrate them already."

Just as I was about to give Edgar a high-five, a pickup truck driving down the road skidded to a stop. The driver jerked the truck into reverse, backing right up to the gate.

"Uh oh," I said under my breath.

"What's wrong?" Edgar asked.

"That's Denton's truck."

Sure enough, the driver's door flung open, and Denton stepped out. He charged toward the gate, letting out a stream of cuss words. "You had no business telling the police I was mixed up in that guy's death," he yelled from the other side of the gate. "They had me there the whole night!"

"Why did they release you?" I asked, my voice shaky.

"Because I have an alibi, you dumb broad!" Denton clenched his fists. "There's no way I could have killed that man. I was at the roller rink the entire night, and I can prove it!"

***

"It's nice to see Thor looking so relaxed," Grandma said to me and Hudson.

The three of us were sitting at a table in the Prairie Dog Lodge later that evening, having just finished a delicious prime rib dinner. It was a celebration of sorts. Once I had confirmed with Leif that Denton did indeed have an alibi, we realized my grandfather hadn't been the intended murder victim after all. And that meant that whoever the killer was, their target had been Wolf all along. Grandpa was safe. No one wanted him dead.

I glanced over at my grandfather, who had wandered off to sit at the adjacent bar with a couple of his buddies and shoot the breeze.

Turning to smile at my grandmother, I asked, "So, no more pickles needed?"

"Pickles?" Hudson asked with a quizzical expression on his face.

Grandma laughed, then explained about the emergency quest for bread and butter pickles earlier in the day. "He ate so many of them when I got back from the store that it gave him a tummy ache. I think he'll be avoiding pickled vegetables for quite a long time."

The server came over to clear the table. When she told us the dessert special was New York style cheesecake, Edgar immediately came to mind. "Can I get a piece to go?"

After the confrontation with Denton, I had brought Edgar back to the library. As I was letting him out of the tapestry bag, he complained that he didn't have anything to snack on during the showing of *National Treasure*. When I pointed out that the library staff served popcorn when they showed movies, the chameleon fussed about how the kernels got stuck in his teeth. In order to shut him up, I promised to bring him a snack sometime soon. Cheesecake would be the perfect treat.

While my grandmother and Hudson ate their dessert, I asked what they thought the next steps in our investigation should be.

"Investigation, dear?" Grandma set her fork on her plate. "But the case is closed as far as we're concerned. Denton didn't try to kill your grandfather."

"But *someone* was killed in his barn," I pointed out. "I think we have a duty to keep going and find out who the murderer is."

"I agree with Thea," Hudson said. "We can't just let this go."

My grandmother thought about this for a moment, then nodded her head. "Okay. Let's call this meeting of the Three Investigators to order."

Reaching into my purse to pull my notebook out, I said, "The first thing we should do is make a list of who had a motive for wanting Wolf dead."

"We did that the other day." My grandmother dabbed her lips with a napkin. "The only person we identified was Kayla."

"And she has an alibi," Hudson said.

I shrugged. "Alibis can be broken."

Hudson tilted his head to the side. "Are you saying the police didn't check her alibi thoroughly?"

"I'm saying we should do a little quality control." Turning to a fresh page in my notebook, I scribbled down some action points, then read them out loud to the others. "One—find out Kayla's alibi. Two—confirm Kayla's alibi."

"Seems pretty straightforward," Hudson said.

"Leif didn't know what Kayla's alibi was originally. At the time it didn't matter because our focus was on Denton." I sighed. "But we should have followed up on it. It was sloppy on our part."

Grandma shook her head. "You can only work with the information you have. And our information pointed to Denton."

"It's an easy enough fix now though, isn't it?" Hudson turned to me. "Why don't you text Leif and ask him to find out?"

While we waited for Leif to respond, I suggested we widen our pool of suspects. "Grace Ryan is someone we should look at too. She was determined to make national news with an article about the 'Whymonstrosity.' Grandpa refusing to be interviewed by her was a real problem for the paper. But maybe publishing photos of the ball of twine would have been enough to get her the coverage she wanted."

"Are you saying Grace could have snuck into the barn to take pictures?" Hudson made a stabbing motion with his fork before continuing, "and then took matters into her own hands when Wolf caught her?"

I nodded. "Exactly."

"Don't forget the arrangements Grace made with Kayla before Wolf put the kabosh on it," my grandmother pointed out.

"Yeah, I still wonder what that was all about," I said. "If Kayla didn't kill her boss slash lover, she might have some useful information about Grace. We should chat with Kayla about it when we check up on her alibi."

"Um, I don't recall us saying anything about having a chat with Kayla," Hudson said slowly, eyeing me. "If she did kill Wolf, confronting her could be dangerous."

"That's right, dear," Grandma said. "Checking her alibi doesn't necessarily mean we need to speak with Kayla."

"Maybe. But first, we need to know what her alibi is, and after that, decide what to do. Okay. Everyone happy with that approach?" I looked down at my phone. "Why hasn't Leif responded yet? Oh, wait, there he is."

Out for drinks right now. I'll get back to you.

Putting my phone back on the table, I said, "Well, that's not very helpful." I gave my grandmother a mischievous smile. "Ooh, do you think he's with a girl?"

Before she could reply, Hudson jumped in. "A girl from his training course? Aren't the participants from all around the country?"

"I think so. Why?"

"Long-distance relationships are hard." As Hudson scraped the last of the cheesecake off his plate, he added, "Might be easier if he met someone closer to home."

"It is hard when the person you're interested in is far away," I said quietly.

Hudson shot me a look; his fork poised in front of his mouth. After setting the fork back on his plate, he said softly, "It helps to be face-to-face, so you can work through things together."

We held each other's gaze until my grandmother cleared her throat. "Thea, dear, can you go ask your grandfather if he wants the rest of my cheesecake? I can't eat it all."

"Sure," I mumbled, suddenly eager to get away from the table.

My grandfather was sitting in the corner of the bar with a couple of guys he used to go pheasant hunting with. As they were swapping stories, Ivan Koslov walked up holding a pitcher of beer. He winced as he put weight on his right foot. "Shouldn't have done those leg curls today," he muttered to himself. A smile spread across his face when he spotted me. "Thea, I hoped I would run into you."

I smiled back. "How are you, Ivan? I didn't expect to see you here."

Ivan set the pitcher down on the table. He moved his hands under his chin, doing the perfect impression of a prairie dog surveying its territory. "We stand by our burrow mates through thick and thin."

After everyone else at the table chimed in with a rousing, "Yip, yip, yip!" one of Grandpa's buddies got up and slapped Ivan on the back. "Ivan is a fellow Prairie Dog, visiting us all the way from Alaska."

"Wow, I didn't realize there was a lodge in Alaska," I said.

My grandfather's buddy grinned. "One day, there'll be a lodge in every state."

As Ivan poured beer for the guys, I noticed that his head was free of cuts and nicks. Maybe he had finally mastered the art of shaving his head. I couldn't say the same about his jeans. That distressed look had never been my thing, but its popularity never waned over the years.

"Can I get you a glass?" Ivan asked me.

Pointing at the table where my grandmother and Hudson were sitting, I said, "No thanks, I'm only here for a minute."

After Grandpa passed on finishing up my grandmother's cheesecake, I asked Ivan what was happening with his book.

Ivan shook his head. "I've decided to change tack. I think poetry is more my thing."

"So, no great American novel about twine?"

"Haiku has my heart now. Here, let me read you one." Ivan reached into the backpack sitting next to his chair. As he pulled a leather journal out, a bunch of papers and envelopes went flying all over the place. When I tried to collect them, Ivan refused my help. "No, I'll get them." He gave me a nervous laugh. "Some of my correspondence is private."

Once he had restored everything back into his journal, Ivan gave me a hopeful look. "Ready?"

"For ..."

"One of my poems," Ivan gushed as he flipped through the pages of his journal. "Here it is. An ode to coffee." He proceeded to recite his very odd coffee-alien haiku mashup: "Cold coffee in space. It's how aliens wake up. Caffeine first, then fly."

I clapped my hands politely.

"Want to hear another one?" Ivan asked eagerly.

"Um, sure." I looked around the table to see what the guys thought about Ivan's impromptu poetry reading. But their expressions were all blank.

"Okay. Ready?" Ivan cleared his throat. "The little green men. So grateful, caffeine, it's why aliens invade."

"Come on, time for a toast," one of my grandfather's buddies interjected quickly. As they lifted their glasses in honor of absent Prairie Dogs, I wondered to myself if anyone was mourning the loss of Wolf. Maybe Kayla was, but what about Wolf's wife?

As I walked back to the table in a more somber mood, I noticed my grandmother and Hudson were engaged in what appeared to be a very serious conversation. I really hoped it wasn't about the status of my relationship with Hudson. I wanted to figure that out with him, alone. Good thing Norma wasn't here. Imagine the field day she would have had trying to get the skinny on whether love was in the air between us.

Love? I mentally shook myself. Please, let's not be thinking about romance. You haven't even kissed the man yet. Love wasn't remotely in the equation. Was there even an equation at this point? No 'one plus one equals two.' The only number that added up here was three, as in the Three Investigators. And that's what we should be focused on—investigating Kayla's alibi and checking to see if Grace was a suspect.

Grandma waved me over. "Thea, come over here. We have something important we need to discuss with you."

"What's that?" As I sat down, I looked back and forth between the two of them.

Hudson leaned forward. "If we're going to try to break Kayla's alibi, there's someone else's alibi we should be looking into as well."

I put my hand to my mouth. "You're talking about Denton, aren't you? That means you think we still need to be worried about Grandpa being a target."

CHAPTER 10
TO DRY OR NOT TO DRY?

Before we left the lodge, I managed to get a hold of Leif. After a quick interrogation about whether he had been out on a date—no surprise, Leif invoked the Fifth Amendment and refused to talk—we got an answer to one of our most pressing questions. Kayla's alibi was Ingrid Ragnhild.

You could have knocked me over with a feather when Leif told me that. Ingrid, the cashier at the Little Pickle, had vouched for Kayla. The two women were together the entire night, from eight until well after eleven. According to Leif's buddy on the police force, Ingrid had made a food delivery to the rental place where Kayla and Wolf were staying. The ladies had ended up hanging out for the rest of the evening.

Unfortunately, this was where Leif's information dried up. Had Ingrid and Kayla known each other before? If not, why did the two of them spend all that time together? Generally, when a stranger delivering food shows up to your house, you thanked them, gave them a tip, and waved goodbye. Inviting them in to hang out—that's a little strange.

Leif did have one other important thing to tell us. And no, it wasn't about who he was dating. Although, believe me, I tried to get that out of him repeatedly. Leif's news was about Denton. Apparently, he'd headed out of town shortly after his confrontation with me at the farm. The annual Dehydro-Con was taking place in Miami, and Denton was a featured speaker. His topic sounded scintillating 'To Dry or Not to Dry? Strategies for Dehydrating Oversized Objects.'

Since the police could confirm that Denton had boarded a flight to Miami, that meant it was safe for my grandparents and me to return home for the night. After a surprisingly restful night's sleep, I woke up the next morning to find Grandma in the kitchen taking some cookies out of the oven.

"When I get back from church," she said to me, "let's take these cookies over to Kayla."

After pouring myself a cup of coffee and adding a generous splash of half-and-half, I asked if that was a good idea. "Remember what Hudson said last night? If Kayla did kill Wolf, it might be dangerous for us to confront her."

My grandmother furrowed her brow. "But we're just bringing her cookies."

I chuckled. "So, arming ourselves with baked goods is going to keep us safe? I gotta tell Leif that one. He can trade in his service weapon for a cheesecake or something."

"Don't be silly, dear. It's not about arming ourselves," Grandma explained. "We're simply paying Kayla a friendly visit. An old lady and her granddaughter? She won't see us as a threat."

Looking at the cookies on the cooling rack, I said, "But Kayla's gluten-free. She won't be able to eat these."

"Don't worry, I made them especially for her. Instead of regular flour, I used almond flour. They're also peanut free. They do have chocolate chips in them. No one can resist chocolate chips."

"Especially for breakfast ..." I reached for a cookie, but my grandmother batted my hand away. "I hope Kayla is in a sharing mood," I grumbled.

Resigned to toast and peanut butter for breakfast instead of cookies, I popped some bread in the toaster. "Shouldn't we talk to Ingrid first?"

"I thought about that," my grandmother admitted. "But I think we should hear what Kayla has to say, and corroborate it with Ingrid."

"Makes sense." I unscrewed the cap of the peanut butter jar. "Ingrid doesn't have any skin in the game. She wouldn't have any reason not to tell us the truth."

My grandmother nodded. "Exactly my thinking. If Kayla lied about what happened that night, hearing Ingrid's version of the story afterward could help us uncover what really happened."

Sitting down at the kitchen table with my breakfast, I asked, "Where's Grandpa?"

"He drove into Williston. The barn is still off limits, leaving him without a place to putter around in. He was feeling a bit at loose ends, so I gave him a shopping list. You know how he loves to wander around the warehouse store. It will keep him occupied for hours."

"Oh, darn it," I said, setting down my coffee cup. "I meant to ask him about the gate."

Grandma joined me at the table with her latest cross-stitch project. "What about the gate?"

Realizing I had never told her about the piece of torn denim Edgar and I found on the barbed wire fence yesterday, I ran upstairs and brought down the tapestry bag. Returning to the kitchen, I opened it up, pulling out the fabric along with the Three Investigators book.

"*The Mystery of Monster Mountain*. Looks interesting," she said, examining the book's front cover. "Where did you get it?"

"At the library."

She turned the book over and pointed at the price tag. "Oh, I see. You bought this. Good for you. All the money that's raised from the used book sales really helps the library out."

Guilt washed over me. What was it that Edgar had said? 'It's only stolen until you pay for it.' I sighed. First thing tomorrow morning, I was going to head to the library and fork over the money for *The Mystery of Monster Mountain*. I made a mental note to bring the piece of cheesecake in the fridge along with me for Edgar.

"What's it about?" my grandmother asked, flipping through the pages.

"I'm not sure," I confessed. "Edgar wants me to read it, but I haven't had time yet."

Grandma tapped the cover of the book. "If your guide told you to read this, there must be something important in here," she said firmly. "It's not long. You can read it tonight. Okay?"

Pushing the crust from my toast around my plate, I muttered, "Yes, ma'am."

"Good. Now what is it you wanted to know about the gate?"

Grateful for the change of subject, I unwrapped the tissue and showed her the piece of fabric, being careful not to touch it directly with my fingers. "My theory is that when Denton climbed over the gate the night Wolf was killed. His overalls got caught on the barbed wire fence, tearing this off. I planned to give it to the police, but then we found out Denton had an alibi. Or at least, we think he does. We still need to check it out."

My grandmother took a sip of her coffee. "Are you and Hudson still going to the roller rink this afternoon to see if you can break Denton's alibi?"

"Uh-huh."

"Hmm."

Half-curious what that 'Hmm' meant and half-fearful it was a precursor to questions about what was going on between Hudson and me, I said brightly, "You should come with us."

Waving a hand in the air, Grandma chuckled. "Roller skates and I are a bad combination." She took another sip of coffee before she asked, "What are you going to do with that fabric?"

"It's evidence, so I suppose I should give it to the police. I'll tell Leif about it first," I said. "To be honest, having overlooked it isn't a great look for them."

"Hmm."

Fortunately, this 'Hmm' appeared to be directed at the police, not at me and Hudson.

"That's where my question about the gate comes in," I said. "If the gate had been open when the police arrived, they might have assumed the killer drove onto the property through the gate, rather than climbed over it. It would explain why they missed the fabric."

"Oh, I can answer that," Grandma said. "Before your grandfather went to get donuts early that morning, he told me he'd unlocked the gate and left it open. He knew folks would need access later for the judging and reception."

Grandma's expression sobered as soon as those words came out of her mouth. "Poor Thor," she said softly.

"Don't worry," I said with more confidence than I felt. "Once the killer is behind bars—"

My grandmother set her cross-stitch down. "*If* we ever figure out who the killer is."

"Hey ... of course, we will." I got up to refill her cup and add half-and-half. After setting it back down in front of her, I continued, "We only have three suspects—Denton, Kayla, and Grace—how hard can it be?"

This made her laugh. "Seems fitting considering we're the Three Investigators. Although I'm not sure how we can tie Grace to the murder."

"We already have a possible motive—animosity toward Wolf when he wouldn't let her cover the 'Whymonstrosity' in *The Daily Why*," I pointed out. "We just need to make sure she doesn't have an alibi."

Picking up her cross-stitch again, my grandmother said, "I find it interesting that this case is all about motives and alibis, not about how the murder was committed. That aspect is really clear-cut."

"That's true. Whoever was in the barn had access to the murder weapon. It's not like a poisoning case where you have to figure out how the killer got the poison, let alone how they knew how to use it."

"Don't forget how important the coroner is in poisoning cases," Grandma added. "Some poisons can make it seem like the victim died naturally."

I gave an involuntary shudder as I recalled finding Wolf's body. No one could doubt his death was anything other than foul play.

Grandma and I sat quietly for a few moments, then I took my dirty plate over to the sink. After rinsing it off and putting it in the dishwasher, I pulled a plastic bag out, and placed the tissue containing the fabric scrap inside it for safekeeping. Grandma looked up from her cross-stitch again.

"Why don't I give Leif a call about the fabric before I head out for church?" she suggested.

"Fine by me." I smiled. "Maybe you can get more information from him about who he was out with last night?"

After handing the bag to her, I went to put my 'stolen until you pay for it' book back into the tapestry bag. "Hang on, there's something else in here." I pulled out a flashlight and groaned. "I forgot about this."

Grandma gave the flashlight a curious look. "Was it in the tapestry bag when you found it in the attic?"

I shook my head and explained how I had grabbed it off a hay bale when Edgar and I were in the barn. "The lights still weren't working, so I used this to look around."

"Last night, you said there wasn't much to see," she said as she sorted through some embroidery floss.

"Well, that wasn't exactly true," I said slowly. After taking a deep breath to steel myself, I blurted out, "Someone tried to destroy the 'Whymonstrosity.' Grandpa's been through so much already, and he was enjoying himself at the lodge last night. I didn't want to ruin things for him, so I, um ..." I ran my fingers through my hair, not sure what to say.

The blood drained from Grandma's face. She put a hand to her heart and spluttered, "Destroy Thor's ball of twine ... Who? How?"

Seeing how devastated my grandmother was made my heart sink. This was exactly what I had been trying to avoid by keeping what had happened to myself yesterday. But now that the cat was out of the bag, I plowed ahead, describing the damage I had seen. "It's only one small section that was destroyed, not the entire ball." As an afterthought, I added, "Leif must not have known about it, otherwise he would have said something."

My grandmother pressed her lips together. "How could someone do something like that?"

"Because they're a monster," I spat out, tightening my grip on the flashlight. "That's why I still think it was Denton. He's the only person who would have wanted to destroy the 'Whymonstrosity.' We have to break his alibi."

"You're going to break that flashlight if you're not careful," Grandma said evenly.

Looking down, I realized my knuckles were white. "Here, take it."

My grandmother examined the flashlight. "Did you see the initials engraved on this? 'GMR'."

Bending over her shoulder to get a look, I asked, "What's Grace's middle name?"

"I'm not sure."

"Do you think it could start with the letter 'M'?" Sinking down into the chair next to my grandmother, I added, "Maybe Denton didn't do it after all."

My head was starting to hurt from all the jumping back and forth between suspects. First Kayla, then Denton, and back to Kayla before jumping to Denton again. And now Grace was taking center stage.

"This could be evidence that Grace was in the barn that night taking photos," I said. "She could have dropped her flashlight when Wolf caught her there—"

"Then she grabbed the pruning shears and stabbed him in the back," my grandmother said, her voice rising in pitch. Grabbing her phone from the table, she announced, "We need to call Leif now."

***

A police officer came by the house not long after my grandmother spoke with Leif. It was the same guy who had asked for my phone number the day of Wolf's murder. Later he had avoided making eye contact with me while I was cooling my heels in the interview room at the police station. Given his previous hot and cold behavior toward me, I wasn't sure what to expect from him now.

"The chief told me to give you a message," he said, as his opening line.

"Okay," I said slowly. It probably wasn't going to be an invite for a girls' night out on the town.

"She wanted me to remind you that police tape isn't a suggestion. It says, 'Crime Scene—Do Not Cross' for a reason. Emphasis on the 'Do Not Cross.'"

"Okay," I said again, this time with surprise in my voice. Chief Jeong's message was much more pleasant than I'd expected. I had trespassed onto the crime scene, which was how I found the flashlight. She would have been within her rights to throw the book at me. I breathed a sigh of relief at getting off so lightly.

The officer shuffled his feet. "That's not actually how she put it," he admitted. "But I don't like cussing in front of ladies."

I smiled at him. "I appreciate it. Let her know, message received."

After handing him the flashlight and scrap of fabric, the officer lowered his voice. "Between you and me, the reason she's not throwing you in a jail cell is because one of the rookies picked up the flashlight and put it on that hay bale. It should have been logged as evidence."

Feeling sick to my stomach for the poor rookie, I said, "What's going to happen to them?"

He shook his head. "Nothing good." He tipped his hat and returned to his squad car.

While my grandmother was at church, I took the dogs outside to play fetch, making sure to keep our distance from the barn. When she got back, we packed up the cookies, and headed across the street to pay a visit to Kayla.

She looked surprised to see us, clutching the sash of a silk robe around her waist as she opened the door. Her face was make-up free, and her hair was wet, as though she had just gotten out of the shower.

"We come bearing cookies, dear." Grandma held up the plate.

"Oh, um, that's nice of you." Kayla held out her hand to take the cookies from my grandmother. "You didn't need to do that."

"We should have done it sooner," Grandma said, still clutching the plate. "You poor thing, sitting here in this house all by yourself after your boss was brutally murdered. It's really inexcusable on our part not to have come by to pay a condolence call before now."

"Don't worry about it. A condolence call isn't really necessary. Wolf was my manager. It's not like we were family or anything." Kayla reached out her hand again for the cookies. "Here, let me take these from you. I'm sure you have a busy day you need to be getting on with."

"Nonsense. It's Sunday. Our schedules are completely open." My grandmother turned to me. "Isn't that right, Thea?"

"Sure," I replied, omitting the fact that I was due to meet Hudson at the roller rink in a couple of hours.

"Then that's settled." My grandmother slipped past Kayla. As she walked inside the house, she said over her shoulder. "We'll get some coffee on while you get dressed, dear."

Kayla gave me a knowing look. "My granny is the same way. Lonely old ladies, am I right? You have to humor them."

I nodded conspiratorially, then followed Kayla into the house. I certainly wasn't going to correct her impression of my grandmother. I had read enough Miss Marple mysteries to know people were more willing to open up to meek-looking old ladies.

By the time Kayla returned to the living room, wearing leggings and a baggy tunic with her damp hair pulled into a loose ponytail, the coffee was ready. As Kayla sank onto the couch, my grandmother placed a tray of cookies on the coffee table.

"The chocolate chip cookies on the right are the ones I made," Grandma told Kayla. "I found the others in the kitchen."

Kayla shook her head. "I can't eat those."

My grandmother held up her hands. "No, you can. Don't worry. I used a gluten-free recipe. They're perfectly safe for you to eat."

"It's not just gluten I need to worry about," Kayla said. "I also have a severe peanut allergy."

"Is almond flour okay?" My grandmother asked, concern showing in her eyes.

"Oh, that's fine. It's just peanuts I have to stay away from." She pointed at the cookies on the left side of the tray, "But I know for a fact that those ones aren't gluten free."

Grandma furrowed her brow. "They were in a bakery box marked with a 'gluten-free' label."

"It was mislabeled." Kayla rubbed her stomach. "I tried one the other night and paid the price. I should have thrown them out right away. It's not like Wolf is around to eat them anymore."

Kayla suddenly broke into tears. Wrapping her arms around herself, she sobbed, "What am I going to do without him? He rented this house for two weeks, so we could have some quiet time together after we finished with the ball of twine. But now I'm here all alone."

I grabbed a box of tissues off a side table while my grandmother comforted Kayla. "Oh, you poor thing. You must miss him terribly."

Once Kayla got her emotions under control and wiped the tears from her face, she turned to my grandmother. "I do miss him. We were together … um, I mean, we worked together for two years."

My grandmother patted her hand. "He was more than your boss, wasn't he, dear?" When Kayla started to protest, Grandma added, "It's okay. Wolf told me that he and his wife were separated."

Well, that was a big fat lie. My grandmother had never discussed Wolf's marital situation with him, but I played along. Sometimes, you had to bend the truth a little to get to the bottom of things. And you withheld the truth to try to protect people, like I did earlier, not telling my grandparents about the vandalism of the ball of twine. I was beginning to realize that truth-telling was often a judgment call, and not always an easy one.

"They were getting a divorce. Wolf was going to marry me as soon as it went through. Did you notice that she hasn't even turned up here? She couldn't care less that he's dead," Kayla said, the words rushing out. "His wife wasn't supportive of Wolf's creative side at all. When his career as a commercial director didn't pan out, she wanted him to get a boring office job. He did it for a while, but it about killed him. So, when he had the chance to invest in the McGuinness organization, he jumped at it."

"Because of the dance and song numbers they do?" I asked.

Kayla blew her nose before she said, "Exactly. McGuinness is committed to next level production numbers. They don't simply hand out world record certificates. They create holistic, immersive, fun-filled extravaganzas."

"I can see why you were attracted to Wolf. He was an artist, a free spirit." My grandmother gave a slight frown. "Sometimes men like that can be hard to live with, though. I wouldn't be surprised if the two of you fought sometimes. It's only natural."

"He could be difficult," Kayla sniffed. "But I still loved him."

"Of course you did, dear. And I'm sure he loved you." My grandmother smiled at Kayla. "When I first saw the two of you together, I could tell you were meant for each other."

Kayla reached for one of the gluten-free cookies. "Really?"

I shot my grandmother a look. Since when did she think it was okay that a married man—separated or not—conducted an affair with another woman? Never was the answer. Not only had I inherited my nosiness from my grandmother, it appeared my ability to bend the truth also came from her.

As if sensing what was going through my head, she motioned for me to go to the kitchen. "Kayla's coffee is probably cold. Can you get her some more?"

When I returned with a fresh cup of coffee, my grandmother had already coaxed Kayla into recounting the events of the night Wolf was killed.

"Wolf had gone to the barn to meet the stage lighting guy and take care of a few other things," Kayla said.

"Did he drive over there?" I asked.

"No, he walked," she said. "He wanted to stretch his legs."

I took a sip of my lukewarm coffee, wishing I had poured myself a fresh cup, too. "About what time was that at?"

"Around seven thirty." Kayla nibbled on her cookie, then turned to my grandmother. "This is delicious."

Grandma beamed at her. Baking for others was a source of enjoyment for her. When they raved about what she made—even better.

"How can you be so sure of the time?" I asked Kayla.

Kayla wagged her finger at me. "You sound just like the police."

Holding my hand up, I said, "Sorry. Guilty by association. My brother is on the force."

"Don't mind my granddaughter. She's nosy." My grandmother chuckled. "She got that from me."

"I didn't mean to pry," I said quickly. "But Wolf met his demise in my grandfather's barn. Naturally, we're interested in what happened. You can understand that, right?"

"Totally." Kayla nodded. "What else do you want to know?"

My eyes widened slightly. Maybe this was going to be easier than I'd thought. "Could you pick up with where you were talking about Wolf having left for the barn, and the time?"

"Yeah. When Ivan showed up, I looked at my phone. It was seven forty, and Wolf had left maybe ten minutes before that. So, that's how I came up with seven thirty."

"Ivan Koslov was here?" my grandmother asked.

"He wanted to talk to Wolf about his contract," Kayla explained. "I told him he had just missed him."

I leaned forward. "So, Ivan went to the barn that night?"

Kayla shrugged. "I'm not sure."

"How long was Ivan here?" I asked.

"Not long. He left before the delivery lady got here." Kayla furrowed her brow. "No, that's not quite right. I'm misremembering things. When the doorbell rang, he asked to use the restroom. I was in the kitchen with the delivery lady unloading the groceries when I heard him call out that he was leaving."

"That's kind of unusual to have the delivery person help unload groceries, isn't it?" I asked. "Normally, they hand them to you at the door, and that's the end of it."

"She offered," Kayla said. "I figured it was one of the perks of living in a small town. They put your groceries away for you."

"It was Ingrid Ragnhild who delivered the groceries from the Little Pickle, wasn't it?"

Kayla sat up straight. "How did you know that?"

I smiled. "Small town, remember?"

"You know, if you had asked me a few days ago whether I would ever consider living in a small town, I would have laughed in your face." Kayla relaxed back onto the couch. "But people are so sweet here, it's made me reconsider big city life. Ingrid was so easy to talk with. It was like we had known each other for years."

"What did you talk about?" my grandmother asked.

"Anything and everything." Kayla giggled as she waved a hand in the air. "That's what happens when you get a few drinks in me."

Grandma smiled at her. "Sounds like the two of you had a nice time."

"We did," Kayla said. "Ingrid and I had a couple of glasses of wine and some snacks. She didn't end up leaving until after eleven. On account of our drinking, you know. Wanted to make sure she had metabolized the alcohol in her system before driving."

"Weren't you worried when Wolf hadn't come back?" I asked.

"At the time, I figured he got caught up getting ready for the next day, wanting to make sure everything was perfect. He is like that ... I mean, he was like that." Kayla's voice wavered as her eyes grew moist. "If only I had known what had really happened ..."

"It's okay, dear," my grandmother soothed softly. "There's nothing you could have done."

"I can't believe your neighbor killed my Wolfie!" she cried out.

As fresh tears flowed down Kayla's face, I handed the distraught woman more tissues. "We're not actually sure that Denton killed Wolf," I admitted, once her tears subsided. "He has an alibi for when it happened."

Kayla whipped her head in my direction. "What? When I went to Dane's Diner the other day, the waitress told me your neighbor was the killer."

"Oh, I think you mean Swede's Diner," my grandmother said. "And Norma isn't necessarily a reliable source of information."

After Kayla had come to terms with the fact that the police still didn't know for certain who had killed Wolf, I asked her if she had any ideas.

While Kayla thought about this, I helped myself to one of the store-bought cookies. They weren't that great. While I was reaching for one of my grandmother's home-made ones, Kayla blurted, "Grace Ryan. That's who did it. She murdered my little Wolfie."

CHAPTER 11
DRIED DINNER

"Grace Ryan murdered Wolf." Hudson let out a low whistle as he tied the laces on his rental roller skates. "Kayla really said that?"

Jamming my feet into my own rental skates, I said, "Her exact words were, 'killed my little Wolfie,' but close enough."

Hudson arched an eyebrow. "Wolfie?"

I shrugged. "Some people give their partners pet names."

"There's this guy back in Coconut Cove who does that. He calls his wife, Mollie, the funniest things, like 'my little rutabaga' or 'my little panda bear.' I think it bugs her."

"Well, yeah. It would bug me, too." As I bent over to adjust my skates, I said, "What are we even doing here?"

Hudson grinned. "Do you mean at the roller rink, or is this a more metaphorical question?"

"The roller rink, silly."

"Is 'silly' your pet name for me?"

"We're not partners," I said matter of fact. "Pet names don't apply."

"Speaking of being partners," Hudson started to say before I cut him off.

"Please, not now." I held up my hand. "I do want to finish our conversation from the other night, but right now we need to concentrate on solving Wolf's murder."

"Which is why we're at the roller rink." Hudson got up and tested his skates. "To answer your previous question."

"I know why we're at the roller rink," I said, a touch exasperated. "What I meant is, why are we putting on skates?"

"Because we have time to kill. Sorry, probably not the best turn of phrase."

Hudson pulled me to my feet, his hands lingering on my forearms longer than needed. Thankfully, I had my favorite University of Minnesota sweatshirt on. Its thick material meant I couldn't feel Hudson's fingers touching my skin, which was good. Checking Denton's alibi was my priority, not thinking about Hudson's physical proximity to me.

"The girl who was working with Denton the night Wolf was killed won't be in for an hour," Hudson continued. His fingers slid down my arms and took hold of my hands, sending tingles down my spine. "That gives us plenty of time to do some skating."

As he led me to the rink, Hudson asked for more details about the conversation my grandmother and I had with Kayla earlier in the day. Glad to be talking about murder rather than my feelings for him, I gave Hudson a quick recap as we glided around the rink together. "Wolf walked across the road to the barn around seven thirty. Ivan Koslov arrived at the Larsen's place at seven forty to talk with Wolf about his contract."

"Ivan was there?"

"Uh-huh. The guy seems to pop up everywhere these days. I certainly didn't expect to get a poetry recital from him last night at the lodge." I made a detour around a couple of young kids with their dad and caught back up to Hudson. "Based on the delivery app tracker, Ingrid arrived with groceries for Kayla and Wolf at eight on the dot. Ivan left shortly after that. Ingrid stayed until after eleven."

"Did Kayla explain why Ingrid was there for over three hours?" Hudson asked. "It's kind of odd to invite a stranger into your home, don't you think? Or did they know each other previously?"

"No, they didn't know each other. How could they have?" Lowering my voice, I said, "Based on all the empty wine bottles I saw in the kitchen, I suspect Kayla had already been drinking quite a bit before Ingrid arrived. She was probably a bit tipsy and happy to have someone to talk with."

"But what about Ingrid?" Hudson asked. "Doesn't she have other things to do on a Friday night?"

"I don't always have plans on Friday nights." I maneuvered my skates into a stop and leaned against the wall of the rink to catch my breath for a minute. "Not everyone has a hectic social life."

"I didn't mean going out on the town necessarily," he said. "Personally, my idea of a perfect Friday night is reading a good book by the fire."

I smiled at him. "Same." The mood changed for a moment between us, but I broke the spell. "I don't really know Ingrid, other than seeing her at the grocery store or on the theater stage."

"She's an actress?"

"At the community theater. They're doing *The Music Man*. My grandmother and I are planning to go see it. Want to come with us?"

"Sure. I'd love to join you."

Bobby Jorgenson banged on the glass barrier separating the roller rink from the rest of the skating center. "That girl, Tammy, you wanted to talk to is here early."

As Hudson and I skated off the rink, Bobby asked why we wanted to speak with Tammy. My instinct was to snap, 'None of your business,' but I bit my tongue. Bobby and I had a long history, and none of it good, dating back to elementary school when he picked on me non-stop. He was also known as the town's local good-for-nothing, often unemployed and always looking for a loan, a frequent flyer at the local bars, a chain smoker, and an all-around jerk.

Well, that was until recently, when he got a job at the roller rink as a skating instructor. No one was more surprised than me to find out Bobby was good at teaching people how to skate. Not only that, but he had managed to hold down this job for more than a month, which was probably his personal best.

"It's about my grandfather," I ended up explaining to Bobby.

Bobby scratched his chin. "Oh, yeah? How's the old man doing?"

"Okay."

"That was pretty rough what happened to him," Bobby said.

I cocked my head to the side. "Do you mean Wolf Shafer's murder?"

"Huh? Oh, you mean the dead guy."

"Generally, when someone is murdered, they end up dead," I said, rolling my eyes.

"Suppose so." Bobby shrugged. "But I was talking about the 'Whymonstrosity.' Shame they canceled the world record thing. You know, I can measure it, if you want. Gotta just tie a few dozen tape measures together, but other than that, should be a piece of pie."

"I think you mean cake," I said.

Bobby nodded. "Cake is good."

"Where is Tammy?" Hudson interjected.

"Over there at the jerky booth." Bobby pointed at a woman in her early twenties standing behind a rickety booth that looked as if a carpenter had made it with his eyes closed and one arm tied behind his back. A hand-painted sign hung from the top, which read, 'Dried Meat.' Probably not the most appealing way to draw customers in.

"Is that Denton's?" I asked.

"You betcha. He's been selling his jerky at the rink for a couple of weeks now. Tammy helps work the booth." Bobby made a finger gun gesture at Hudson, pretending to shoot him. "You should probably stay away from the stuff given your sensitive stomach."

I looked at Hudson. "You have a sensitive stomach?"

"Not really," he said.

Bobby chortled. "Man, the way you ran to the bathroom the last time you were here says differently."

"What are you talking about?" I asked Bobby.

"Do we really have to discuss it?" Hudson held up his hand. "I shouldn't have had that chili dog, okay? It was embarrassing."

"I'm so lost here," I said.

Hudson's face reddened. "Come on, Thea. Remember when we were here on our first date and I had to leave early. Bobby told you that I was sick."

"Bobby didn't tell me anything," I said, shaking my head slowly.

Hudson turned to look at Bobby. "When I saw you in the men's room, I asked you to give Thea my apologies. Didn't you do that?"

I glared at Bobby. "No, he didn't."

"Sorry, man, I forgot," Bobby confessed. "Anyway, gotta skate. Private lesson starting soon."

Hudson stared after Bobby, his teeth clenched. He turned back to me. "I'm so sorry, Thea. You must have thought I was such a jerk running out on our date like that. Then the next day I rushed off to Florida, and we never really had a chance to talk ..." He looked down at the floor, and continued, "Correction, I didn't make time to talk with you."

"I'm just as much at fault in this as you are." Tilting Hudson's chin up, so that he was looking at me, I said, "I could have tried reaching out more when you were in Florida. You were going through such a hard time with your uncle. I could have been a better friend to you. But I assumed the worst about you, thinking that you had ditched me here at the roller rink."

"Can we have a do-over?" Hudson asked softly.

It was all I could do not to throw myself into Hudson's arms and brush my lips against his own. But I wanted our first kiss to be a private moment, not something witnessed by everyone at the roller rink. Instead, I simply said, "Yes." After a beat, I added, "To be continued?"

Hudson nodded. "You're right. Let's focus on the murder investigation." He pointed at the jerky stand. "Shall we?"

Our conversation with Tammy turned out to be a bust. She swore up and down that Denton had been working the booth with her the entire night. Some of the other regular customers at the rink backed her up too.

"We were slammed," she explained. "There wasn't any time for either of us to get a break."

"That many people wanted to buy jerky while they're roller-skating?" I asked.

"This isn't just any jerky," Tammy explained, her voice full of passion. "This is specialty jerky."

Hudson examined the packets on display. "What makes it so special?"

"Flavor. It blows my mind how Denton packs all that flavor into each piece of dried meat." She picked up one of the packets and tore it open. "This is Denton's latest invention, 'Dried Dinner.' Three pieces of jerky are in each packet. The first one tastes like a wedge salad with blue cheese dressing," she said, indicating a piece with a greenish hue. "The next one is the main course—tater tot hotdish. And to round things off," continued Tammy as she pointed at a blue-colored piece of jerky, "blueberry pie. Here, try some. On the house."

"I think I'll pass." Hudson grimaced as he rubbed his stomach. "I already learned my lesson about eating at the roller rink."

After we managed to extricate ourselves from Tammy's sales pitch, we went to return our skates. After we got into our street shoes, Hudson asked what our next steps were in the investigation since we had crossed both Denton and Kayla off our list of suspects.

"Don't be so fast crossing off Kayla," I said. "We still need to confirm her alibi with Ingrid. Grandma and I are going to swing by the Little Pickle tomorrow afternoon to have a chat with her and see if there are any inconsistencies in Kayla's story."

"That leaves us with Grace," Hudson said. "How should we tackle that?"

"Are you talking about Grace Ryan?" Bobby Jorgenson asked as he skated up to us out of nowhere.

"Maybe," I said. "Why?"

"Did you know teaching people to skate is like being a therapist ..." Bobby said, skating circles around. "Or a bartender? Or a hairdress—"

"I thought we were talking about Grace," I interrupted and yanked Bobby's arm, bringing him to a stop. "You are making me dizzy," I said by way of apology.

Bobby looked down at my hand, and I pulled it away. As I wiped it on my jeans, he teased, "Afraid of cooties?"

"Knock it off and get to the point," I huffed.

"Okay, as I was saying, everyone tells you their problems when you're out on the rink." Bobby gave me a cocky grin. "Wanna tell me yours?"

I punched Bobby in the arm. "You're my problem."

"Kids," Hudson said in a warning tone. "Play nice or I'll send you both to the timeout corner."

"Chill, man," Bobby said to Hudson. He turned back to me. "A couple of nights ago there was a guy in here who used to work for Grace. She fired him because he wouldn't report bake news."

"Bake news?" I furrowed my brow. "Do you mean fake news?"

Bobby thought about that for a moment. "Fake news … oh yeah, that makes more sense. Anyway, he had a lot to say about Grace. None of it good. She's a power-hungry witch, according to him. Cut-throat." Making a slashing motion across his neck, Bobby added, "Like, literally, cutting throats. You wouldn't believe what she said about the dead guy."

Hudson and I both leaned in, eager to hear what Grace's ex-employee had said. Instead, Bobby started skating circles around us again. Only this time, it was Hudson who pulled Bobby to a stop.

"Tell us what the reporter said," Hudson demanded.

"That Grace would kill anyone who got in her way of a big story, including the McGuinness dude," Bobby said before skating away.

***

It's always a challenge keeping up with my day job when we're in the midst of an investigation. Being self-employed means I have some flexibility in my schedule, but not complete control. Working around my client meetings on Monday morning meant I didn't get to the library until lunchtime.

I made sure to bring two essentials with me—cheesecake for Edgar and money to pay for *The Mystery of Monster Mountain*. It was amazing how quickly the guilt washed away from me as I transformed my 'it's only stolen until you pay for it' book into a 'you paid for it, now you own it' book. It probably didn't hurt that I told the library assistant to keep the change from the twenty I handed to her. I considered it to be a sort of tax for my guilty conscience.

After metaphorically wiping my hands clean, I went in search of Edgar. "Cheesecake, here," I whispered in my best imitation of a quiet carnival barker. "Genuine New York style cheesecake here."

The resulting 'Whoosh' (trademark pending) nearly gave me whiplash. Edgar landed on my shoulder, crying out, "Cheesecake! Hand it over, lady!"

"Get inside." I held up the tapestry bag. "Let's have a picnic in front of the library."

After we were situated on a bench outside, I pulled the container of cheesecake out for Edgar, along with a ham sandwich for myself. I had barely opened the box when Edgar crawled inside and started chowing down. Gingerly setting the box on the bench so as not to disturb his feast, I asked him how it was.

Edgar poked his head out, licking cream cheese off his mouth. "Fantastic, lady. Where did you get it?"

"The Prairie Dog Lodge."

"You gotta get me more. This is the best thing I've eaten since moving to North Dakota."

"It was a special," I explained after taking a bite of my sandwich. "I'm not sure when they'll have it on the menu again."

Edgar groaned as he ducked back inside the box to lick up the last crumbs of cheesecake. When the chameleon was done, he hopped out and perched on the back of the bench. After letting out a belch that stunk to high heaven, he announced, "Okay, time to call book club to order."

Fortunately, I had managed to read *The Mystery of Monster Mountain* last night when I got back home from the roller rink. "I thought the vegetarian character was interesting." Looking down at the remnants of my ham sandwich, I asked, "Could you ever give up meat?"

"No way, blondie. Hot dogs are my favorite food group." It took me a moment to register that Edgar had one of his eyes pointing at me, with the other turned in the opposite direction to look at something else. I guess I was getting used to the little reptile's physical peculiarities.

"Did you figure out why I wanted you to read the book?" Edgar asked.

"Um, not really," I admitted. "Is it because you want me to take you to a ski lodge?"

"No, dummy," he said. "Do I look like I would enjoy careening down a mountain on a couple of planks of wood? I could break my neck."

"You could try snowshoeing instead," I suggested. "Or curl up in front of the fire with a good book."

"If you want to go on a romantic getaway with Hudson, leave me out of it."

I furrowed my brow. "Who said anything about a romantic getaway?"

"Back to the book, lady. What did you think about the character who—"

Before Edgar could finish his thought, Ivan came rushing toward us, his backpack bouncing up and down on his back. When he reached the bench we were sitting on, Ivan stumbled. The man landed on the ground with his journal clutched in his hands.

"Keep that—that beast away from me," Ivan spluttered as he crawled under the bench and cowered.

"Can he see you?" I whispered to Edgar.

"I'm not a beast!" Edgar snapped.

"Is he gone?" Ivan asked, his voice trembling.

"There's no one here but me and … I mean, it's just me here," I said.

Ivan pulled himself out from under the bench and sat down next to me, slinging his backpack on the ground. He was breathing heavily, and his bald head was covered in sweat.

Feeling uncomfortable, I scooted down towards the other end of the bench. My discomfort was twofold. Sitting that close to a strange, sweaty man gasping for breath was certainly off-putting. But also, something in the back of my mind niggled at me. Had Ivan been in the barn the night Wolf was murdered?

While Ivan wiped his brow with his hand, I thought it through. Ivan had gone to Kayla and Wolf's rental place to speak with Wolf about his contract. Kayla had told him that Wolf wasn't there and where Wolf was, presumably.

I tapped my fingers on the bench's armrest. So, had Ivan gone across the street to talk with Wolf? And if that was the case, what exactly did he want to discuss regarding his contract? Was he unhappy with the terms? I remembered Wolf saying he was going to pay Ivan in kind for his work as a documentarian. But what did that even mean? McGuinness merchandise like hats, t-shirts, and that kind of thing, perhaps? But probably not as satisfactory as cold, hard cash.

Looking over, I saw Ivan muttering to himself as he leafed through his journal. Something green flickered, catching my eye. "Hey, can I see that?" I asked.

Ivan cocked his head at me. "See what?"

"That envelope. It looks familiar."

"Oh, that's nothing," Ivan said with a nervous laugh. He snapped his journal shut. "Just something I scribbled poetry on."

I was about to question him further when I felt someone squeeze my shoulders. Looking up, I saw Hudson standing there.

"I saw you earlier in the library, but didn't get a chance to say hi," he said to me. He walked around the bench and extended his hand to Ivan. "I don't think we've met before."

When Ivan wiped his hands on his jeans before shaking Hudson's hand, I shuddered. Was it better that Ivan wiped the sweat off his hand first or worse that he used his grimy jeans to do so?

Suddenly, my heart began to race. The jeans Ivan was wearing were ripped and tattered. Most of the rips and tears were intentional, part of the distressed look some people thought was fashionable. But could one of those rips and tears be the result of Ivan catching his pants on a barbed wire fence?

After the guy delivering the stage lights had left, Wolf had locked up the gate behind him. If Ivan had gone to the barn to talk about his contract with Wolf, he would have had to climb over the gate. All this time, I had assumed the torn denim fabric I found was from Denton's overalls. But what if it had come from Ivan's jeans?

I tried to send Hudson a telepathic message—*Be careful. Ivan could be the killer*. Though since I don't have any telepathic abilities, he was oblivious to what I was trying to say. When the library had given me the magical ability to see an invisible chameleon guide, why couldn't it have bestowed some other useful gifts at the same time, like telepathy or teleportation? Imagine how much money I would save on gas if I could instantly transport myself to my destination rather than having to drive everywhere.

While Hudson and Ivan chatted away about poetry, I put a few other puzzle pieces together. The envelope I spotted in Ivan's journal was dark green, the same color as the envelope Wolf had shown us in the kitchen right after he had completed his preliminary measurements of the 'Whymonstrosity.'

Ivan had wanted to witness Wolf measuring the giant ball of twine, but why? At the time, he had told us it was research for his great American novel about twine. But after Wolf's death, he suddenly abandoned his novel in favor of poetry. And based on the poems he had recited at the lodge, they featured aliens drinking coffee, not verses about twine at all. Why the sudden shift in literary focus?

"Hey, lady, don't forget about *The Mystery of Monster Mountain*," I heard Edgar say in my ear.

"That's it," I cried out, slapping my leg.

Hudson turned to look at me. "What's it?"

"Hidden identity. That's why he wanted me to read ..."

"Who wanted you to read what?" Hudson asked, looking perplexed.

I shook my head. "Sorry. I meant hidden identity is a key plot point in the Three Investigators book I read last night."

Ivan shoved his journal in his backpack before he got to his feet. Jostling Hudson out of the way, he said, "You know, I need to get going."

"You're not going anywhere," I said, trying to block his path.

Ivan's eyes grew wide. Clutching his backpack to his chest as though it was protective armor, he shrieked. "The beast! It's back!"

Hudson turned to look at what had frightened Ivan so much, then chuckled. "That's no beast. That's—"

"No, you should be scared of that buffalo," I said, cutting Hudson off. "He's a very scary beast. If you don't tell us the truth, he'll gore you with his horns, and break all your bones with his hooves."

"Whoa, Thea! What's gotten into you?" Hudson asked. "Bufford wouldn't—"

I shot Hudson a look, hoping he would understand what I was doing. Maybe I had some limited telepathic abilities after all. Hudson nodded and said slowly, "That's right, Bufford is a scary beast."

"Hand me your journal," I said to Ivan.

Ivan's hands were trembling as he pulled the journal out of his backpack and passed it to me. I leafed through the pages until I found the dark green envelope.

"What is that?" Hudson asked.

After explaining what it contained, I said, "The gold wax seal is missing. Ivan removed it so that he could find out how big my grandfather's ball of twine is." I opened the flap of the envelope and pulled out a piece of heavy cream-colored card stock. After examining what was written on it, I handed it to Hudson.

He looked at the number written on the card, and asked, "Is this good or bad?"

"Honestly, I don't know." I narrowed my eyes and looked at Ivan. "But I'm betting you know the answer to that."

"I—I don't know ... what you're talking about," Ivan spluttered.

I turned and nodded at Bufford. He obliged by stamping his hoof and snorting angrily.

So much sweat was pouring off Ivan's head and into his eyes that I wondered how he could see. With his body shaking uncontrollably, he said, "Please don't sic the beast on me. I'll tell you anything you want to know."

"Let's start with where you're really from," I said. "When I first met you, you said you lived in Florida. But on Saturday night at the lodge, one of the guys said you were from Alaska. Which is it?"

After some gentle coaxing by Bufford, Ivan choked out, "A-Al-Alaska."

"And do you happen to have your own ball of twine up in Alaska?" I asked.

"Yes," Ivan admitted softly.

I folded my arms across my chest. "Hoping to get your own world record by any chance?"

Ivan nodded. He sank back onto the bench, his shoulders slumped. "I've been working on it for years. I practically rubbed my fingers raw tying on so much twine. When I heard the McGuinness organization was coming to North Dakota, I got worried. The world of giant balls of twine is very competitive, you know."

"Huh. Competitive twine balls. Who would have thought?" Hudson murmured.

"You have no idea how much it would mean to me to get the world record for the largest ball of twine," Ivan said, his eyes glistening with tears.

"That's why you came here and posed as a writer. You wanted to get friendly with the McGuinness organization, so you could see how much of a threat my grandfather's ball of twine was to your own." Grabbing the card from Hudson and waving it in the air, I added, "I'm guessing from this, the 'Whymonstrosity' is bigger than your ball of twine. Or should I say, it was until you vandalized it!"

When Hudson clenched his fists, Ivan shrank back on the bench. At that moment Bufford rushed forward, and Ivan put his head in his hands and cried out, "I confess. I did it. Please don't let the beast eat me!"

CHAPTER 12
THE BEAST

Hudson and I watched as the police officers escorted Ivan to the squad car. Correction: There were actually four of us watching Ivan's arrest—Hudson, Bufford, Edgar, and I.

Bufford quickly got bored though, opting to chew on the grass growing in front of the library instead. Edgar grumbled about how hungry he was from his perch on the back of the bench. How exactly did a tiny chameleon fit so much cheesecake in his belly and still have room for more? Yet another mystery to be solved. But for now, I was going to be satisfied with what we *had* solved—Ivan Koslov slashed my grandfather's ball of twine. When Wolf caught him in the act, Ivan stabbed him with the pruning shears when his back was turned to keep him quiet.

"I never thought Bufford would be our heavy," Hudson said after the squad car with Ivan in it pulled out of the parking lot.

Bufford snorted in response and shuffled over to join us. "Can you believe Ivan thought you would eat him?" I cooed in the buffalo's ear as I scratched his neck. "A sweet, gentle beast like you."

One of the police officers walked up to us, nodding at Bufford in acknowledgment of his contribution to apprehending the murderer. Maybe the mayor would award the buffalo some sort of medal of commendation.

"When we handcuffed Mr. Koslov, he vehemently denied killing Wolf Shafer," the officer said.

"Of course he did," I scoffed.

The officer nodded. "He admitted to vandalizing the 'Whymonstrosity,' though."

Hudson sighed. "I suppose he's holding off on confessing to murder, hoping he can cut a deal with the D.A."

"Not my department," the officer said. "Anyway, thanks for your help. Give us a minute to take your formal statements, then you're free to go."

After the police were done with their paperwork, I looked at the time on my phone. "Yikes, I'm late."

"Work stuff?" Hudson asked.

"No, I'm meeting my grandmother at the Little Pickle."

"Oh, right. The two of you were going to confirm Kayla's alibi with Ingrid," Hudson said. "Guess you can call that off now."

I nodded. "Still, I'm going to head down there. For some reason, I have a sudden craving for pickles."

Hudson gave me a funny look. "Pickles? Usually when a woman craves—" Then he chuckled. "Of course you're not, um, never mind."

"Okay, this conversation is getting weird," I said with a smile. "I'm going to get going."

"Are we still on for *The Music Man* with your grandmother?" he asked.

"Yep, we have tickets for the show on Friday night."

Hudson frowned. "So, am I not going to see you for the rest of the week?"

"I'm sure we can work something out."

Hudson and I made plans to have a midweek dinner at the local Chinese restaurant, and he headed back to the library. I gathered up the tapestry bag along with the trash from my picnic with Edgar.

"Can I come?" Edgar asked.

"Back to the library?" I opened the tapestry bag and waited for him to jump in. "Of course. I'm not going to leave you out here."

"No, I meant to dinner with you and Hudson. I'm having a craving for pork lo mein."

I shook my head. "No way, buddy. But if you behave yourself, I'll bring you back some leftovers."

I let Edgar out of the bag in the entryway to the library, then headed to the Little Pickle. When I got there, Ingrid and my grandmother were sitting at a table in the little cafe section of the grocery store.

"Oh good, you're here," Grandma said when she spotted me. "Let me get you a cup of coffee."

"Actually, I think I'll pass on the coffee," I said.

My grandmother stared at me. "Are you feeling okay, Thea?"

"Yeah, I just want something cold." As the cashier was ringing up my iced tea, I noticed a poster for the community theater production hanging on the wall. It showed the stars of the show—Ingrid and a firefighter whose name I couldn't remember. Ingrid, who was playing Marion, the town librarian, was dressed in a long-striped skirt, a high-neck blouse, and a short green jacket with a straw hat on her head. The firefighter looked sharp in the plaid suit he was wearing and made a convincing Professor Harold Hill.

While I waited for the cashier to find a wedge of lemon for my tea, I tried to recall *The Music Man's* storyline. The professor had posed as a salesman, selling musical instruments and band uniforms to the unsuspecting residents of River City. Eventually, he was discovered to be a conman, but confessed what he had done, earning Marion's forgiveness.

Was it possible for a criminal to turn over a new leaf and redeem themselves? In my heart, I believed in forgiveness and redemption. Forgiving a conman, like those gutter salesmen who had skipped town, seemed plausible. But when it came to a murderer who had struck way too close to home—in this case, literally right next to the house I lived in—it was harder to accept. Could I forgive Ivan for what he had done? Maybe someday, but that day was a long way off.

After squeezing the lemon into my iced tea and giving it a stir with my straw, I went to join Ingrid and my grandmother. As I sipped the cool lemony liquid, my body relaxed. Instead of talking with Ingrid about Kayla's alibi, the three of us could simply have a friendly chat.

"How much longer is your break, dear?" my grandmother asked Ingrid.

Ingrid glanced at the clock on the wall. "I've got another fifteen minutes. But there's no rush. It isn't busy in here, and the junior cashiers can cover things. The store manager practically has me running the place when he isn't here."

The man who had been stocking the shelves the other day and bad-mouthing Ingrid walked by at that exact moment. Based on the look he shot Ingrid, I was pretty sure he had overheard what she said. Ingrid didn't appear to be well liked by her fellow employees.

"Oh, good," my grandmother said to Ingrid. "Since you have time, I'd love to hear more about what it was like working in Hollywood."

Ingrid leaned forward, clearly eager to tell us about the glamour and glitz of life on the big screen. After sharing a few stories that sounded like they came straight out of a gossip magazine, Ingrid said, "Grace Ryan is actually going to do a feature on me in *The Daily Why*."

"Really? About your Hollywood days?" I asked.

"That's right," Ingrid said. "When she pitched the idea to me originally, she wanted to focus on the production of *The Music Man*. But I told her she would sell more copies of the paper if she wrote about my Hollywood days. When she gets back from New York later this week, we're going to do a whole photo shoot."

"Grace is in New York?" I asked.

"Uh-huh. She's meeting with some high-flying finance guys about investing in the paper. Her vision is to make *The Daily Why* the preeminent newspaper in the Dakotas. There's even talk about making it a daily publication rather than weekly."

"That certainly would have made Grace's father happy," my grandmother said. "It had been his dream to have a daily paper."

"Do you know when Grace went to New York?" I asked idly. Now that Ivan had been arrested, it didn't really matter where Grace had been at the time of Wolf's murder. But it would be nice to tie up any loose ends. And there was still the open question of how Grace's flashlight had ended up in the barn. Assuming the initials 'GMR' engraved on it meant it belonged to her, of course.

"She left on Wednesday night," Ingrid said. "I know that because she came into the Little Pickle on her way out of town to get some snacks for the plane. We talked about the photo shoot."

I mentally reviewed the timeline—Wolf had been killed on Thursday night, which meant Grace hadn't been in town at the time. But when and how could she have left her flashlight in the barn?

Ingrid leaned forward. "I shouldn't say this, but Grace was furious that you wouldn't let her write an article on the 'Whymonstrosity.'"

While my grandmother was explaining exactly why Grace was a persona non grata, a police officer walked into the cafe. Realizing it was the same guy who had picked up the flashlight and scrap of denim fabric the other day, I gave him a small wave.

He did a double-take when he saw me. "Wow, did you hear the news?" he asked after getting a soda to go.

"About Ivan Koslov's arrest for murder?" I asked. "Yeah, I was there."

My grandmother put her hand on my arm. "Ivan was arrested. When did this happen?"

"Sorry," I said. "I didn't have a chance to tell you. It was right before I came over here. He admitted to vandalizing Grandpa's ball of twine."

"Did he admit to killing Wolf?" Ingrid asked.

"Not yet," I said. "But it's only a matter of time. He's obviously guilty."

Ingrid looked off in the distance. "Wow," she said softly.

The police officer cleared his throat. "I was actually talking about the woman who passed away across the street from you."

"Do you mean Kayla Goodwin?" my grandmother asked.

The police officer nodded. "Yes, ma'am."

Ingrid's eyes widened. "Oh, my gosh. That was the gal I delivered groceries to the other night."

"No, that can't be right." Grandma put her hand on her chest. "Thea and I just saw her yesterday. We brought her cookies. When did this happen?"

"I'm not sure," the officer said. "The cleaners found her this morning."

"Do you know what the cause of death was?" I asked.

The officer shook his head. "No, I don't."

"Sorry, I couldn't help but overhear." I turned and saw the junior cashier, who had given Ingrid the evil eye earlier, standing there. "Are you talking about the lady who's staying at the Larsens' place?"

Ingrid frowned. "John, you should get back to work. Those shelves aren't going to stock themselves."

John rolled his eyes at Ingrid as he shifted the carton in his arms. Looking back at the police officer, he said, "It's just that I made a delivery to her last night. She was perfectly fine then."

"Let me get your name," the police officer said to John. "We might want to get a statement from you. It's possible you were the last person to see her alive."

As the officer took John's details down, I looked at my grandmother. "I can't believe it. Two deaths on our road in less than a week."

Grandma shook her head. "Those poor souls. Kayla and Wolf, visitors to our quiet town, both ending up dead. What are the chances?"

***

By the time Friday night rolled around, I was ready for a relaxing weekend. Going to see *The Music Man* with my grandmother and Hudson was going to be a good way to kick that off.

"You ladies look nice," Hudson said when we walked into the lobby of the community theater.

My grandmother was wearing a floral skirt, pastel-colored cardigan, sensible heels, and one of her trademark scarves around her neck. I had traded in my usual everyday casual wear for something a bit fancier—a cornflower blue shift dress, dangly earrings, and not-so-sensible shoes. It wasn't often that I wore heels since leaving my corporate job, so donning them tonight made this seem like even more of a special occasion.

"You look pretty spiffy yourself," I said, taking in his well-tailored navy suit. "I don't think I've ever seen you in a tie before."

"The last time I wore one was when I was interviewing for the library director role," Hudson admitted. "But since we're out for a night on the town, I figured it was a good opportunity to wear a tie. It's a shame Thor didn't want to join us."

While we waited for the doors of the theater to open, Hudson asked if there was any update on Ivan's case.

I nodded. "Leif got back into town yesterday afternoon. Naturally, he made a beeline for the house when he heard Grandma was making pulled pork. While he was stuffing his face, we managed to get a few bits of information from him."

"Oh, that's right. He was away on a training course. How did it go?" Hudson asked.

"Pretty good." I looked around to make sure we wouldn't be overheard. "He has an interview with the sheriff's office next week."

Hudson tilted his head. "If he gets the job, do you think Chief Jeong will be happy or sad to see Leif leave?"

Grandma chuckled. "Hard to say. She'll resent the sheriff poaching Leif, but she might also be thrilled not to have an Olson working for her."

"Well, I hope it works out for him." Hudson rubbed his hands together. "Anyway, tell me what Leif said about Ivan."

"Why don't you start with Kayla first?" my grandmother suggested.

"Yeah, the poor girl," I said. "Turns out she died from anaphylactic shock, a severe peanut allergy."

Hudson frowned. "Usually, people who have food allergies like that are really careful about what they eat. And they have an EpiPen handy."

"Unfortunately, not in this case," I said.

"It wasn't Kayla's fault. She ate a cookie from a box that said it was peanut-free, but it turns out it had peanuts in it." My grandmother shook her head. "I feel bad for the owners of the Little Pickle. People are going to be hesitant about buying things from their bakery when they hear about what happened. There might even be liability issues."

"Is it an on-site bakery?" Hudson asked.

"Uh-huh," Grandma said. "They advertise the fact that all the baked goods they sell are made from scratch."

"So, they would have put the labels on the boxes themselves," I mused and furrowed my brow. "Don't you think it's strange that Kayla had that happen to her twice? The first time was the night Wolf was murdered. She had cookies delivered from the Little Pickle that turned out to have gluten in them."

"That's right, dear," my grandmother said. "I had forgotten about that."

"Remember how Kayla said she had eaten some of them that night? She said she had 'paid the price.'"

Hudson rubbed his stomach. "I know what that's like. After that chili dog at the roller rink, I was in and out of the bathroom the entire night."

"So do you think—" But before I could finish my thought, the doors to the theater opened, and we took our seats. My grandmother was so busy introducing Hudson to the people seated next to us that we didn't get to continue our conversation.

The curtain went up, and we were treated to a lavish—by small town standards—production of *The Music Man*. While my grandmother and Hudson appeared enraptured by the song and dance numbers during the first act, I couldn't help but think about the deadly cookies Kayla had ingested. When the lights went up for intermission, I started to excuse myself.

"Are you going to the ladies' room?" my grandmother asked. "I'll go with you."

I ran my fingers through my hair, undecided about whether to tell her what I was really planning to do. After a beat, I said. "No, you go ahead. I need to talk to Hudson about something."

After my grandmother walked toward the restroom, I grabbed Hudson's arm. "Come on, let's go."

"Where are we going?" he asked as I dragged him toward a door marked 'Performers Only.'

"Backstage," I said. "Come on."

"Hey, you can't be back here," a man yelled at us.

"Yes, we can," I said over my shoulder as we darted around a pile of props. "We're from the library."

The man furrowed his brow. "Oh, okay."

"The library?" Hudson asked.

"Worked, didn't it? It's all about projecting confidence." Realizing we had passed our destination, I grabbed Hudson's hand and backtracked a few feet. "Here we are."

Hudson looked at the door we stood in front of. It was adorned with a large gold star with the name 'Ingrid Ragnhild' on it. "Shouldn't we wait until after the show is over to say hi?"

"Nope, no time like the present." I rapped on the door, then pushed it open without waiting for an answer.

"What if she's changing?" Hudson asked, putting his hands over his eyes.

"Thea, what are you doing here?" Ingrid was sitting at her dressing table, touching up her makeup. "And who's that handsome gentleman behind you? It's okay, honey, I'm decent."

Hudson tried to introduce himself to Ingrid, but I stopped him. "No time for pleasantries."

"That's true," Ingrid said as she adjusted the microphone attached to her wig. "The curtain is going to go up in a few minutes. We're having a reception after the show. Why don't you come say hi then?"

"That sounds like a good idea." Hudson tugged at my elbow as he smiled brightly at Ingrid. "I loved your performance of 'Goodnight, My Someone.' Your voice is stunning."

Seeing how Ingrid beamed at Hudson's compliment, I decided to modify my approach—less confrontational, more sucking up.

"Hudson's right. You're amazing on stage. Everyone seated next to us was saying the same thing." I lowered my voice. "I don't know how you can stand to perform with all these amateurs, though. They're singing off-key, and half of them can't remember their lines."

Ingrid nodded. "I've tried my best to work with them, but it's a struggle. That dumb firefighter playing opposite me is the worst. Someone should tell that man about breath mints."

"They're beneath you," I said, trying my best to ooze sympathy. "A star like you belongs in Hollywood, not North Dakota."

"You're preaching to the choir, sister." Ingrid turned back to the mirror, fussed with her wig some more, and touched up her lipstick.

I chose my next words carefully, wanting to lull her into a false sense of security. "If it weren't for Wolf Shafer, things would be different, wouldn't they?" Crossing my fingers that she would take the bait, I added, "Wolf was like the character of Professor Harry Hill in *The Music Man*, right? He conned you out of your savings, didn't he?"

Ingrid slammed her lipstick down on the dressing table. Turning toward me, her eyes flashing with anger, she snapped, "That's exactly what he did. I was only nineteen at the time, and he promised that if I invested my savings into making a demo commercial, offers for TV shows and movies would come flooding in."

"He took advantage of you," I said softly.

"And my money," Ingrid said bitterly. "He took all my money. I didn't have any choice but to come back home with my tail between my legs and take a stupid cashier job at the Little Pickle."

"It must have been a shock when you saw Wolf again." I glanced over at Hudson, noting his frozen expression. I bet he wasn't expecting this when I dragged him backstage. Turning back to Ingrid, I said, "Did Wolf come into the Little Pickle? Is that when you saw him?"

A lone tear fell down Ingrid's cheek. "The man didn't even recognize me."

"Five minutes to curtain," a voice said over the loudspeaker. "Ladies and gentlemen, five minutes to curtain. Please take your seats."

Ingrid dabbed at her face with a tissue. "I need to get ready for the second act."

"Sure, but there's one other thing I wanted to know," I said evenly. "When did you decide to kill Wolf? Was it premeditated? Or was it a spur-of-the-moment thing when you made that grocery delivery to the place Wolf and Kayla were renting?"

I heard Hudson gasp, but didn't turn to look at him. Instead, I pressed Ingrid further. "My money is on spur-of-the-moment. You had the perfect alibi, didn't you? Spending the evening sipping wine and snacking with Kayla. Except she ate something that didn't agree with her—cookies with gluten in them. So, while she was in the bathroom, suffering, you took the opportunity to run across the street to the barn. You confronted him about what he had done. Then you killed him when he turned his back on you. Isn't that right?"

Ingrid got to her feet, brandishing a hairbrush. "Wolf deserved to die. It's not just me whose life he destroyed. There were other girls he conned. I did it for every single one of them. You should thank me. The world is a better place without Wolf Shafer in it."

Someone knocked on the door, interrupting Ingrid's tirade. She yelled at them to go away. But instead, the door opened slowly, and the man playing Professor Hill poked his head through. "Um, Ingrid, everyone can hear you. Your mic is on." He tugged at his bow tie nervously as he said, "Were you rehearsing a new play? It sounded very dramatic."

Ingrid pulled her wig off. After yanking the microphone from the wig, she tossed it on the floor and smashed it into smithereens with her foot.

The actor looked taken aback. "Maybe I should get the stage manager."

"You should get the police," I said. "In fact, let me dial 911 now."

As I was pulling my phone out of my purse, Ingrid lunged at me. "This is all your fault. I would have gotten away with it if you hadn't stuck your nose where it doesn't belong."

Hudson pulled Ingrid back before she could strike me with the hairbrush. While she continued to yell a stream of obscenities in my direction, I phoned the police.

"What just happened?" the actor asked after I ended the call.

"Ingrid just confessed to murder, and thanks to her open mic, she broadcast her confession to everyone in the theater." Turning back to Ingrid, I said, "I hope you have a good understudy, because you won't be going back on stage. You're going to jail!"

CHAPTER 13
DO NOT EAT RAW POTATOES

The following weekend there was cause for celebration. Two criminals were behind bars, Ivan Koslov and Ingrid Ragnhild. Ivan's vandalism of the 'Whymonstrosity' was certainly a serious crime, but it paled in comparison to what Ingrid had done. Anyone could understand Ingrid's anger at Wolf Shafer. He had conned her out of her life savings when she had been a young struggling actress in Hollywood, forcing her to return home with her tail between her legs. But killing Wolf years later as retribution? Well, that was something I would never be able to wrap my head around.

But the fact that justice had been served wasn't the only reason why the Olson household was bubbling with excitement on Saturday morning. Later this afternoon, a crowd was going to descend on the farm to watch the first ever Why record setting event. The 'Whymonstrosity' was going to be officially measured by the mayor. Considering there weren't any other giant balls of twine in the vicinity, odds were the 'Whymonstrosity' would soon be declared 'The Largest Ball of Twine in all of Why.'

Instead of my grandmother shouldering the burden of feeding everyone, some of the guys from the lodge were going to grill, and everyone else was bringing a potluck dish to share. Grandma was planning on making those adorable twine ball cake pops again, along with a few other dishes. She just couldn't help herself. The atmosphere in the kitchen this morning was much more relaxed than it had been when we were prepping for the arrival of the McGuinness representatives.

"Uff da," my cousin Freya said as she sank into one of the chairs at the kitchen table. "I can't seem to get comfortable these days."

"Well, you are seven months pregnant," I pointed out. After getting Freya some herbal tea, I settled into the chair next to her with a cup of coffee. I asked how the rest of the nursery decorations were going.

"The old rocking horse you found in the attic is the perfect finishing touch," Freya said. "It makes the room look so cozy."

"Don't you think it looks like a Dala horse?" I asked, referring to the iconic carved Swedish horse statues. Traditionally, they were painted in a warm reddish-orange hue. "I wonder if someone in our family made it."

"It would have to be someone from Grandpa's side of the family, wouldn't it? Wasn't someone in his family tree originally from Sweden? I can't remember." Freya took a sip of her tea. "You know, I've always wanted to learn more about who carved the troll statue. Maybe the same person made both of them."

"We should ask Grandma about it," I suggested.

"Ask me about what?" Our grandmother bustled into the kitchen with the dogs on her heels. After explaining we were curious about the history behind the rocking horse and the giant troll by the barn, she smiled at us. "You girls really should learn more about your family history. But not today. Right now, I need your help with the potato salad."

After getting us set up with a huge bag of potatoes, Grandma left us to it.

While we were peeling and chopping potatoes, Freya said, "You know, I don't remember seeing that rocking horse in the attic before. Has it always been up there?" She held a partially peeled potato and pointed at the bag sitting on the floor. "Or that. You said you found that in a trunk, Thea?"

"Uh-huh. It's handy for carrying my laptop and work papers around." What I left unsaid was that it was also handy for transporting snarky chameleons from New York on field trips. For some reason, Edgar wasn't able to leave the library on his own unless he hitched a ride in this particular tapestry-lined bag.

"Hey, lady, pass me one of those potato chunks."

I resisted the urge to turn around and look at Edgar, who I knew was sitting on the windowsill behind me. He had insisted on attending today's event, probably because he knew grilled hot dogs were on the menu.

It had been tricky making the arrangements to transport him here since the library didn't open until ten on Saturdays, and I was needed back home before then to help out. Unlike employees, library volunteers like me didn't have keys to the building. You'd think the library would have thought things through beyond a magic standpoint—if you're going to bestow a mysterious guide on someone, and provide a transportation device in terms of a tapestry bag, the least you could do would be to set up an entryway that didn't require the use of a key.

Thankfully, Hudson planned on catching up on work bright and early this morning, so he could attend the event later this afternoon. Armed with the pretext of bringing him coffee and a Danish, I left the library ten minutes later with a chameleon in my bag.

"Did you know it's bad for you to eat raw potatoes?" I asked Freya, hoping Edgar would get the hint.

Freya wrinkled her nose. "Not to mention tasting gross."

"You know, come to think of it, I think potatoes are toxic to reptiles. Something about the nightshade family."

"Aww, you do care," Edgar crooned.

What I wanted to say back to Edgar was, 'It's more that I don't want to deal with taking you to the vet when you get sick from eating raw potatoes. Imagine trying to explain that I want them to treat a magical chameleon.'

But since Freya was sitting next to me, I zipped my lips and concentrated on the potatoes instead.

"Thinking of getting a snake?" Freya asked, oblivious to the fact that a chameleon kept butting into the conversation.

I laughed. "Pigs would have to fly before I willingly got a reptile."

"Too bad, blondie," Edgar said. "You're stuck with me."

Freya pointed her potato peeler at me. "Hey, I've been meaning to ask you to take me through what happened from start to finish with Grandpa's ball of twine and the murder. My brain is like mush these days, and it's all kind of a blur."

"I'm not sure where to begin." As I set my knife down on the cutting board, Edgar jumped down from the windowsill onto the table. "Watch it. You could get hurt," I cried out.

"Huh?" Freya furrowed her brow, confused.

"Um, yeah," I glared at the chameleon while I tried to figure out what to say. "That potato peeler is sharp. Be careful you don't cut yourself."

"Tell her about Ivan's fake identity," Edgar said.

I shrugged. It seemed like a reasonable starting point. Turning to Freya, I said, "Remember that weird little man, Ivan Koslov. He has his own ball of twine in Alaska. Apparently, news travels fast in twine ball circles. So, when he heard the McGuinness organization was coming to see the 'Whymonstrosity,' he panicked. He came to North Dakota determined to make sure Grandpa's ball of twine didn't eclipse his in size."

Grandma walked back into the kitchen holding a laundry basket. "Are you talking about Ivan? Tell Freya about his fake book."

"The first day Ivan was in town, he went to the library to use the Wi-Fi. He overheard someone saying that Grandma used to be the library director. He decided to pretend to be a writer, thinking that would give him an in with our family."

"Wait, wasn't his supposed book about twine?" Freya looked off into the distance, and said, "Seven hundred and forty-six, right?"

"Very good, dear. I'm glad to see you still know your way around the Dewey Decimal system," my grandmother said. "That's where you'd find books on textile arts shelved at the library. But Ivan was supposedly writing a novel, so you would most likely find his work in the fiction section."

I chuckled. "Doubly so since his book was a complete work of fiction."

After Grandma took the laundry down to the basement, I told Freya how Ivan had latched himself onto Wolf, getting an unpaid gig as a documentarian. "What he really wanted was to be there when Wolf did the preliminary measuring of the 'Whymonstrosity' to see how it compared to his own ball of twine. But Wolf refused, claiming it had to be kept secret."

Getting up from the table to put the cut-up potatoes into a large pot on the stove to boil, I continued to tell Freya about Ivan's deviousness. "Wolf showed everyone the sealed green envelope, which held the answer to Ivan's burning question—how big was the 'Whymonstrosity?' Ivan was desperate to get his hands on it."

Freya lowered her voice. "An awful lot of fuss over twine, don't you think?"

"Don't let Grandpa hear that," I said. "He takes it pretty seriously, too. Anyway, Ivan went to the Larsens' to talk with Wolf about his contract. When Kayla told him Wolf had gone to the barn, Ivan pretended to use the bathroom while Kayla was busy with her grocery delivery."

"Let me guess," Freya said eagerly. "Ivan searched the house for the envelope."

"Bingo."

"Okay, so Ivan opens the envelope and realizes that his ball of twine is smaller than Grandpa's," Freya said. "He went across to the barn after that, right?"

"Yep. Wolf wasn't in the barn at the time. We think he had walked outside to take a call, based on his cell phone records."

"How do you know all this anyway? From Leif? It sure does help to have a brother on the police force."

"He helped fill in some of the details. Of course, you never heard that from me." After Freya mimed a zipping her lips gesture, I told her the general assumption was that Ivan took advantage of being alone in the barn. "He grabbed the pruning shears and started slashing away at the 'Whymonstrosity.' He must have heard Wolf outside, so he dropped the shears and snuck out of the barn before Wolf caught him."

When I glanced over at Edgar, wondering why he hadn't been bothering me with useless commentary, I had to stifle a laugh. The little critter had curled up on a cloth napkin, fast asleep. I think he might even have been drooling.

"So, how did you figure it out?" Freya asked.

I looked up at the ceiling, trying to recall all the details. "Well, it really came down to one big slip-up Ivan made. When I first met him, he told me he was from Florida. But when I ran into him at the lodge, one of Grandpa's buddies mentioned Ivan was a fellow Prairie Dog from Alaska. Ivan had to show his membership card to get into the Why lodge that night."

"Got it. The cards show which lodge you belong to. I bet they kick Ivan out of the burrow," Freya said, referring to the expulsion process for lodge members who didn't adhere to the code of conduct. Vandalizing a fellow Prairie Dog's ball of twine certainly fell into that category.

"You heard that Bufford got Ivan to confess, didn't you?" I walked back over to the stove and gave the potatoes a stir. "That confession tripped me up at first. Originally, I thought Ivan was the murderer, killing Wolf when he was caught in the act of slashing the ball of twine. It never even occurred to me that it was Ingrid."

"Me neither."

"It had been bothering me that Ivan confessed to vandalism, but refused to corroborate killing Wolf. Something in the back of my mind kept thinking, what if Ivan didn't do it? We did have other suspects—Denton and Grace—but ruled them out for various reasons. And we had also eliminated Kayla, because Ingrid had provided an alibi for her."

Grandma walked into the kitchen again, asking how the potatoes were doing. After sticking a knife in one to make sure they were tender, she turned off the stove and drained the pot. "Are you still telling Freya about the investigation?"

"I was about to reveal the connection between cookies and musicals."

"How about some cookies while you do that?" Grandma brought over a container of oatmeal raisin ones, then offered to get Freya some more tea.

Pointing at the cookies, I explained, "These are full of gluten."

"Um, okay." She took a bite and said, "They still taste delicious."

"You know how some people can't tolerate gluten?" I asked. "Well, Kayla was one of them. When she ordered groceries from the Little Pickle, she specified gluten-free cookies. Unfortunately, the wrong label was put on the box."

Freya took another bite of her cookie before asking, "Did Ingrid do that?"

"Not that time." When Freya gave me a confused look, I started explaining how Ingrid had deliberately put the wrong label on the box of cookies that had killed Kayla. "Hang on a minute. Let me back up."

Grandma brought over some tea for Freya and a fresh cup of coffee for me before she busied herself with getting out the rest of the ingredients for the potato salad. Once I stirred some half-and-half into my coffee, I continued, "Ingrid had seen Wolf and Kayla at the Little Pickle the day they arrived in Why. Wolf didn't recognize her, but Ingrid knew exactly who Wolf was—the guy who had conned her years ago. By coincidence, she got assigned the delivery order to the Larsens' place."

"I don't understand why people get groceries delivered," Grandma said. "Especially produce. You really need to pick that out yourself."

"Oof, I'm all for it," Freya said. "Especially with the little one on the way. It'll be such a time-saver."

I smiled. "You guys want to talk grocery delivery or murder?"

"Murder," they both said in unison.

"Okay, so Ingrid shows up at the Larsens' place. Kayla answers the door, and Ingrid decides this is her chance. She's going to confront Wolf. So, she worms her way inside by offering to carry and unload the groceries. Wolf isn't there. However, Kayla has already had a few glasses of wine and is feeling a bit lonely. She ends up offering Ingrid some wine, and the two of them hang out chatting like old friends."

Freya frowned. "I bet Ingrid was trying to get dirt on Wolf."

"Totally. Anyway, the two of them decide to snack on some of the food Ingrid had just delivered, including the cookies."

"The non-gluten-free cookies?" Freya asked.

"Exactly. Kayla had a few of them, ending up with some not so kind digestive issues, shall we say," I said. "While Kayla is in the bathroom for an extended period of time, Ingrid decides to go across the road to have it out with Wolf."

"Kayla had already told Ingrid her boss was over there," Grandma said.

Freya shook her head slowly. "And that's when Ingrid killed Wolf."

"They must have argued. When Wolf had his back turned, Ingrid picked up the pruning shears Ivan had dropped earlier and stabbed him," I said. "Though she had the presence of mind to wipe her fingerprints off them, along with Ivan's."

"Wow, that's cold." Freya cocked her head to one side. "But was Kayla in the bathroom long enough for Ingrid to run across the street, kill Wolf, and get back before Kayla realized she was gone?"

"According to Ingrid, she found Kayla dozing on the couch when she got back. She hadn't realized Ingrid was gone, and Ingrid made it look like she had been there the entire time." I shrugged. "If she hadn't drunk all that wine or eaten those cookies, then maybe she would still be alive."

Freya leaned forward. "So, Ingrid is talking?"

"She wants to cut a deal," I said.

"I think her lawyer might be giving her bad advice," Grandma said. "Sure, the first murder wasn't premeditated, but the second one certainly was. Ingrid was worried Kayla might remember more of what happened that night and realize she couldn't give Ingrid an alibi for the entire time."

"This is where the second box of cookies came in?" Freya asked.

"Yeah. Kayla told Ingrid that night that she was allergic to peanuts. So, Ingrid made a special batch of cookies for her with peanut flour."

"They found the peanut flour in Ingrid's kitchen," Grandma said. "She had put her home-baked cookies in a Little Pickle box, along with a gluten-free label."

"The Little Pickle doesn't use any kind of peanuts in their bakery, so all their boxes say peanut-free already," I pointed out. "The owner's kid has a peanut allergy, so they're really careful about it."

"Ingrid placed an order for groceries using a fake account. When one of the junior cashiers was getting ready to deliver it to the Larsens' place, she slipped the box of cookies inside the bag."

A chill went down my back as I thought about what Kayla's final hours must have been like. She'd eaten the cookies and gone into anaphylactic shock. She didn't have an EpiPen to administer life-saving epinephrine, so she died. The police found Kayla's cell phone under the bed. Maybe she had tried to call 911 for help, but fumbled with the phone, dropping it where she wasn't able to reach it in time.

We all sat silently for a while until I cleared my throat. "There's one other minor loose end we had to tie up."

Trying to lighten the mood, I said with a dramatic flourish, "The Case of the Flashlight."

"Oh, that's right," my grandmother said. "You found that in the barn."

"It had Grace Ryan's initials engraved on it," I explained. "During Grace's discussions with Kayla about *The Daily Why* writing an exclusive article about the 'Whymonstrosity,' Grace had given the flashlight to Kayla as an example of some co-branded merchandise they could do. Apparently, the idea was to have the newspaper and McGuinness organizations' logos engraved on flashlights. Anyway, when Wolf went to the barn that night, he took the flashlight with him."

"The lights keep going out in the barn," my grandmother said as she stirred a mayonnaise-based dressing into the potatoes, along with peas, hard-boiled eggs, and chopped red onion. "I can see why he brought a flashlight that night. They really should have had generators delivered along with the stage lights."

I spread my hands out and smiled at my cousin. "And there you have it, the story behind Wolf's murder."

Freya furrowed her brow. "You also mentioned musicals. What was that about?"

"Ah, the community theater's production of *The Music Man*," I said. "The storyline involves a conman. We knew

Wolf had worked in Los Angeles as a director and that Ingrid had gone to Hollywood hoping to make it big."

"Got it," Freya said. "That's when you put two and two together—Wolf was the conman and Ingrid was his victim."

"Except in the end, it turns out Wolf was Ingrid's victim."

After Grandma put the potato salad in the fridge to chill, she slapped her forehead. "There's something I've been meaning to tell you, Thea. I solved a bigger mystery than who killed Wolf. Remember how your grandfather disappeared?"

"What? Grandpa disappeared?" Freya asked, her eyes wide.

"It was when Wolf and Kayla first arrived. Grandpa went to lock the gate to keep Denton from driving onto the property, but he didn't come back for hours," I explained. "When we asked him about it, he refused to tell us where he had gone."

"Stubborn old man," Grandma muttered.

Freya and I smiled at each other, and I said, "Don't leave us in suspense. Where did he go that night?"

"Denton's farm stand," she said.

"I didn't know Denton had a farm stand," I said. "It's been ages since I've driven past his place."

"I love farm stands," Freya said. "There's one I always go to that has the cutest flower bouquets and delicious jams."

"What does Denton sell at his farm stand that Grandpa had to have so badly that night?" I asked.

"Jerky," Grandma answered. "Thor had a craving for jerky, so he walked down there, put some money in the honesty jar, then sat down under a nearby tree and feasted away. After he polished off the jerky, he ended up dozing off."

"Huh. I guess we have another case to add to our files, 'The Mysterious Jerky Incident.'"

"Well, thank goodness it didn't turn out to be 'Death by Dried Meat.'" My grandmother shuddered. "There's been enough death around here for a lifetime."

CHAPTER 14

WHAT DO A TROLL AND A PIRATE HAVE IN COMMON?

Later that afternoon, anxiety bubbled inside me. Intellectually, I knew my grandfather's ball of twine was the largest in all of Why. How could it not be? The 'Whymonstrosity' was the only one of its kind around. Even so, a million butterflies fluttered in my stomach. What if something went horribly wrong when the mayor measured it?

As if sensing my worry, Hudson took hold of my hand and gave it a gentle squeeze. "Come on, we need to get going."

On our walk from the house to the barn, I stopped to rub the troll's belly. "Troll, can you put in a good word for us? I want to make sure everything goes smoothly for my grandpa."

Hudson started laughing out loud.

I felt my face flush. "What's so funny?"

He immediately started apologizing. "I wasn't making fun of you. I'm sorry. It's just that there's a similar tradition in Coconut Cove."

"You have a troll statue in Florida?"

"Well, not exactly. It's a pirate statue named Coconut Carl in a bar. People come from all around to rub his belly for good luck. I had no idea there was anything like this in North Dakota."

"A pirate and a troll are two very different things," I said with a touch of indignation. A moment later, I started laughing at the ridiculousness of the whole situation. Grown people rubbing carved wooden statues hoping it would bring them good fortune—crazy.

"That reminds me," Hudson said. "I've told you about Mollie McGhie before, haven't I?"

"The one whose husband calls her stupid pet names?"

"That's the one." After taking his phone out of his pocket, he scrolled through his texts. "Here, Mollie sent me a message saying she's going to be in Williston for a FAROUT convention."

"FAROUT?"

Hudson furrowed his brow. "I can't remember exactly what it stands for, but it's basically a group that studies UFOs and alien abductions. I know ... weird, right?"

Not any weirder than being in a book club with an invisible, snarky chameleon and toting him around in a tapestry bag. Of course, I didn't say that to Hudson. Instead, I shrugged my shoulders.

"Anyway, she wants to get together when she's here," Hudson said. "I want to introduce you to her. She's a hoot."

"Sure. After investigating two murders, it'd be nice to talk with someone about something else, even if it is UFOs."

"Oh, about that. Mollie has a tendency to—"

"There you two are." My grandmother walked toward us, waving urgently. "Hurry up, they're about to start measuring."

By the time Hudson and I got to the barn, it was standing room only. Somehow, we managed to wedge ourselves between some hay bales. I took note of the stage that had been set up in front of the 'Whymonstrosity.' My grandparents stood in the center, flanked by the mayor and other local dignitaries. Instead of overalls, my grandfather was wearing a suit, showing how seriously he took this event. But unless the national anthem was playing, no one was going to tell him not to wear his feed store hat.

"Move your big head, lady. You're obstructing my view," a familiar voice said behind me.

"Why don't you move, Edgar?" I said under my breath.

"I was here first, dummy."

Turning around, I eyed the chameleon, who was perched on top of the hay bale directly behind me. He glared back. We continued the standoff until the mayor's booming voice cut across the barn.

"Ladies and gentlemen, please make way for the official measuring team," the mayor proclaimed as though he was announcing the entrance of the athletes at the Olympics.

"I still can't see," Edgar hissed.

Shifting to my right, so that the stupid reptile would shut up, I ended up bumping into Hudson. I started to apologize, but he simply smiled. He put his arm around my waist and pulled me closer.

As the official measuring team marched into the barn, I grinned. Bobby Jorgenson led the procession bearing one end of a series of tape measures that had been duct taped together. Once they reached the 'Whymonstrosity,' Bobby and the other members of the measuring team bowed to the mayor and my grandfather. Next, they proceeded to wrap the patched-together measuring tapes around Grandpa's ball of twine.

Bobby scribbled something down on an index card, then handed it to the mayor. The mayor looked at the card and cleared his throat. "Before I announce the results of the official measurement, I want to remind everyone about the contest. The person whose guess comes closest to the actual diameter of the 'Whymonstrosity' will win a deluxe package consisting of a candlelight dinner at Swede's Diner, an annual pass for unlimited admission to the roller rink, and a hamper full of baked goods donated by Rose Olson. All the money raised will go to the Farm to Food Bank charity."

"Tell us how big it is already," a man shouted.

"Does the hamper include rhubarb cookies?" someone else yelled.

"Settle down, people," the mayor said sternly. After a drumroll by a member of the high school marching band, the mayor revealed the official result.

Applause erupted in the barn, everyone screaming with delight. My grandfather even smiled. Sure, it was a faint smile by most people's standards. But for him, it was practically a grin.

The mayor waved his hands in the air for silence. Once the din died down, he announced the winner of the 'Guess the Size of the 'Whymonstrosity'' contest.

"Denton Watts, you're the lucky winner!" the mayor called out.

My grandmother looked over in my direction, shaking her head. "Figures," she mouthed.

To his credit, Denton shook my grandfather's hand before accepting his prize. Maybe there would be peace between these two men going forward. I just hoped Denton wouldn't try to figure out a way to dehydrate the 'Why-monstrosity.'

"People, quiet, please!" the mayor shouted. "It's time to award Thor Olson with his official certificate. Make way for the official bearer of the certificate."

When Bufford marched up to my grandfather with the certificate between his teeth, Hudson chuckled. "Only in Why, North Dakota."

I smiled. "Sure beats Florida, doesn't it?"

"I think you might be right. But do you know what would make it even better? If we had a do-over on our first date and end it properly ..." Hudson pulled me closer and whispered in my ear, "With a kiss."

THE CARD CATALOG

One of the things I love about writing a library-themed cozy mystery series is sharing my love of all things bookish. Think of this as your personal "card catalog" of some of the books mentioned in *A Death for the Records*.

Were you wondering what romance book Thea was reading in Chapter 1? It was *The Geographer's Map to Romance* by India Holton, a historical fantasy adventure rom-com with a marriage of convenience trope. I absolutely love the witty banter between the two main characters, and Houlton's prose is an absolute delight.

Anna Karenina by Leo Tolstoy doesn't exactly qualify as a romance given its lack of a happily-ever-after ending for Anna and Alexei. But it oozes romance, especially that line Hudson quotes to Thea. Someone recently asked me what books I would reread. Anna Karenina is on that list, for sure.

I love picking up old copies of The Three Investigators books. Reading them takes me back to my childhood. ***The Mystery of Monster Mountain*** by M.V. Carey was a fun one. When the three boys—Jupiter Jones, Pete Crenshaw, and Bob Andrews—take a trip to a ski resort in Sierra Nevada, they naturally stumble across a mystery that only they can solve!

Ray Bradbury's ***The Illustrated Man*** is one of those books that's stuck with me over the years, perhaps because I first read it as a teenager. When I was growing up, I didn't really know many people with tattoos, so the description of a man who had his entire body covered with living, moving images fascinated me. If you haven't read anything by Bradbury before, this is a great collection of short stories to check out.

I'd love to hear about what books you enjoy and whether you've read any of the books mentioned above. Shoot me an email at ellenjacobsonauthor@gmail.com.

Grandma Olson's Recipes

Banana Chocolate Chip Bars

Remember that nice gal whose truck tires were slashed by Denton Watts? Well, this is the recipe she gave to Grandma Olson. It'll satisfy your sweet tooth and then some!

Ingredients:

½ cup (1 stick) butter, room temperature

1 cup packed brown sugar

1 large egg

1 ½ teaspoons vanilla extract

½ teaspoon salt

1 cup all-purpose flour

1 cup mashed ripe bananas (about 2 large bananas)

¾ cup semi-sweet chocolate chips

½ cup chopped walnuts

Directions:

1 – Preheat the oven to 350 degrees.

2 – Line an 8x8 baking dish with parchment paper, then spray with nonstick cooking spray.

3 – Cream the butter and brown sugar together in a large bowl until light and fluffy.

4 – Add the egg, vanilla extract, and salt to the bowl and mix until combined, scraping down the bowl with a spatula as needed.

5 – Add the flour and mix until combined.

6 – Stir in the mashed bananas.

7 – Fold in the chocolate chips and nuts.

8 – Pour the batter into the prepared pan.

9 – Bake for 35-40 minutes until the edges are golden brown and the center is baked through.

10 – Remove the pan from the oven and let cool on a wire rack before slicing.

11 – Hide the remaining bars so that no one else can find them. They're that good!

Tater Tot Breakfast Casserole

Tater tots aren't just for dinnertime. Toss some in your breakfast casserole and watch your family and friends gobble it up!

Ingredients:

1 32 ounce bag of frozen tater tots

1 pound of diced ham

1 small onion

1 green bell pepper

2 cups shredded cheddar cheese

8 large eggs

1 cup sour cream

½ cup milk

½ teaspoon salt

½ teaspoon black pepper

½ teaspoon garlic powder

¼ teaspoon cayenne pepper

Nonstick cooking spray

Directions:

1 – Preheat oven to 375 degrees.

2 – Dice the onion and bell pepper.

3 – Sautee the diced onion and bell pepper in a skillet with nonstick cooking spray until soft.

4 – Spray a 9x13 inch baking dish with nonstick cooking spray.

5 – Place the tater tots, ham, sauteed onions and bell pepper, and 1 ½ cups shredded cheese into the baking dish, stirring with a spoon to combine.

6 – Whisk the eggs, sour cream, milk, and seasoning in a large bowl until combined.

7 – Pour the egg mixture over the tater tot mixture in the baking pan.

8 – Bake in the preheated oven for 45 minutes until golden brown.

9 – Remove the pan from the oven and sprinkle the remaining ½ cup shredded cheese on top. Return to the oven and bake for 5 more minutes until the cheese is melted.

10 – Enjoy!

AUTHOR'S NOTE

Thank you so much for reading my book! If you enjoyed it, I'd be grateful if you would consider leaving a short review on the site where you purchased it and/or on Goodreads. Reviews help other readers find my books while also encouraging me to keep writing.

The inspiration for this book came from seeing the World's Largest Ball of Twine in Cawker City, Kansas. I was utterly in awe of this testament to humanity's quirkiness and knew I had to work it into a book someday. And that day is finally here!

My husband is a proud born-and-bred North Dakotan and the inspiration for this series. I'm eternally grateful to him for his character and story ideas, not to mention his unfailing support of my writing career. Many thanks to my amazing editor, Alecia Goodman, for her thoughtful edits and suggestions.

Find out more about me and my other books at: ellenjacobsonbooks.com.

Stay in touch with my latest book releases and other news by signing up for my free newsletter at: subscribepage.com/m4g9m

ABOUT THE AUTHOR

Ellen Jacobson is a chocolate obsessed cat lover who writes cozy mysteries and romantic comedies. After working in Scotland and New Zealand for several years, she returned to the States, lived aboard a sailboat, traveled around in a tiny camper, and is now settled in a small town in northern Oregon with her husband and an imaginary cat named Simon. Find out more at ellenjacobsonbooks.com

ALSO BY ELLEN JACOBSON

**The North Dakota Library
Mystery Series**

Planning for Murder (prequel)

Murder at the Library

Poisoned by the Book

A Death for the Records

**The Mollie McGhie Cozy Sailing
Mystery Series**

Robbery at the Roller Derby (prequel)

Murder at the Marina

Bodies in the Boatyard

Poisoned by the Pier

Buried by the Beach (short story)

Dead in the Dinghy

Shooting by the Sea

Overboard on the Ocean

Murder aboard the Mistletoe

Mrs. Moto Meows about Murder (short story)

Mollie McGhie Cozy Mystery Collection: Books 1-3

Mollie McGhie Cozy Mystery Collection: Books 4-6

The Complete Mollie McGhie Cozy Mystery Collection

The Smitten with Travel Romantic Comedy Series

Smitten with Ravioli (set in Italy)

Smitten with Croissants (set in France)

Smitten with Strudel (set in Germany)

Smitten with Candy Canes (set in Santa's Village, Finland)

Smitten with Baklava (set in Greece)

Smitten with Caviar (set in Monaco)

Smitten with Tacos (set in Mexico)

Smitten with Travel Collection: Books 1-3

Smitten with Travel Collection: Books 4-6